And Then I Saw You.

A. L. Fox

gemlah

Trigger Warning

There is mention of fertility issues. Some of the complications and emotions that go along with that are voiced throughout. Not heavily, in my opinion, but it is a super small sub-plot. It is not graphic but it may be a something to think about prior to diving in if that is something your beautiful heart is extra emotional towards.

Also, not so much a trigger warning but just a general "hey, here's the thing." This book is not meant for anything other than fun. My entire goal for this story was to be something that makes you laugh. You'll see the dedication in two pages and it's fully that kind of vibe. I kept telling myself as I wrote And Then I Saw You. that I wanted this to feel almost unrealistic. And I think I reached that goal. I love this story, but if you don't enjoy a crazy, wild, unhinged ride just for the sake of a laugh and *swoon,* this may not be the book for you. Just keep that in mind going forward. I don't want you to be mad at me, haha.

Okay, that covers it. Enjoy. xoxo

Playlist

AND THEN I SAW YOU.

Honey, Honey – Mamma Mia Cast
Baby Shark – Pinkfong
September – Earth, Wind & Fire
Time Warp – The Rocky Horror Picture Show Cast
Home – Michael Buble
My Girl – Dylan Scott
I Can Do Better Than That – Anna Kendrick
Right Now the Best – Zach Bryan
Without You – Diplo & Elle King
Santa Baby – Eartha Kitt
Temporary Town – Charles Wesley Godwin
Set Fire to the Rain – Adele
What Hurts the Most – Rascal Flatts
Be Happy – Mary J. Blige
Come Back Home – Sofia Carson
Mom – Garth Brooks

*This one is for anyone who loves
a story that makes them think
<u>"that's fucking insane"</u> and <u>"oh how cute"</u>
in the same breath.*

Contents

Prologue

Take Me to Church

August 2018

Carter

*H*oly shit. Wow.

"What's up, brother?"

I whip my gaze to my buddy, "Huh?"

Ken laughs at me before saying, "You said "wow". I couldn't figure out why." He raises a blonde eyebrow at me.

I did not mean to say that out loud.

"I was looking at that woman down there." I gesture in front of us.

She is gorgeous. Her light blue jeans hug her curvy butt and hips, giving me a good view of just how much there is to hold on to. She's got on this gray t-shirt and even though I haven't seen the front of her yet, I would bet money it has got some bad ass band on the front. Her long brown hair hits the middle of her back and every time she turns her head to talk to the man standing next to her, I notice the bright, cherry red lipstick she has painted on her seemingly perfect mouth.

Ken says something back after seeing who I was talking about, but I can't hear him. No— all I hear is the voice in my head telling me to go to *her*.

"I'll be back, yeah?" I say to Ken as I bend down to grab the back of the gray chair in front of me. I step onto the foldable seat in the row in front of us before jumping down onto the concrete floor of the stadium. Then I begin to finally make my way across the empty row to the stairs that lead down to *her*.

What am I doing?

My feet pause. This is not like me at all. I do not go after women like this. I've been too busy lately— or for the last decade. I hardly even notice the women around me. Taking over a large farming operation will do that to you. But it is what I always dreamed of. Being my own boss has its perks, obviously. But the actual farming aspect? *That* is what gets me. The math that goes behind every planting and spraying season. The science behind it all. The sheer will and faith that comes with a job that is so dependent on weather and nature. The hustle of harvest to beat the cold and wet Midwest conditions that can wreck a good year. All of the hard work, the hand shaking, the ass kissing; it was all worth it.

I stand still for another moment, never taking my eyes off of *her*. Wow, she is beautiful. Seriously, something akin to a goddess. The curl of her hair and the curve of her ass, I would drop to my knees now and worship her if it meant she would just tell me her name.

What the fuck Carter, get it together. You are never like this. About anyone. Ever.

I pull my dark gray Ford baseball cap off of my head and run my hand through my just-long-enough black hair before bending the bill of it a few times and then putting it back on. The need to do something with my hands is damn near overwhelming. I take a deep breath and pull my blue jeans up just to have them settle back on my hips. I am stalling. I kick the heel of my brown cowboy boot on the step behind me before and whisper, "Get it together, man." As I continue my descent I shake my hands out at my sides as if it will help displace some of this nervous energy.

The arena in Sioux Falls, South Dakota is packed to the brim. The parking outside is absolute shit, and the tall-boy Busch Lights are essentially highway robbery in price. But the atmosphere in here is killer and the music tonight is going to be incredible. Eric Church is a fucking master of his craft. This building is massive inside. Two stories with a standing pit area, a lower and upper bowl. We are about smack dab in the middle of the entire arena, a view of the whole place at our disposal. The stage feels pretty far away but even so, EC is good enough it won't matter.

As I get closer to *her* row, I hear her laugh and I find myself pausing my prowling to gain control over myself. Again. This is not who I am. I do not pine. I do not prowl. I do not fucking swoon. I almost never have to make the first move. I am chalking it all up to the fact that she is six rows in front of me therefore she has not had the chance to see me yet. It's the curiosity that is driving me. That's it.

Whatever you need to tell yourself, big guy.

Her laugh... Oh her laugh. It is like a shining light. Not the sunlight, no. It's not something so easily available to the masses. It's like a lighthouse on the coast of an ocean, signaling to a boat trying to get to its dock— a savior. It is like the flashlight you need when you go down in your basement to reset the breakers during a storm— a necessity. Like the warm glow from a fire in the middle of a cut down field, the sky is black, but the stars are bright and plentiful, and the air smells like burnt wood and cut grass— a moment of peace. Her laugh is like that, full and good. Simple but life altering. Familiar in a way I can't explain. And if I am not careful... *earth shattering.*

I inch closer, taking my time because I do not want to fumble this play. Who is the guy she is with? They seem close, she keeps grabbing his arm and shoving her shoulder into his. I have not seen them kiss or anything though so maybe he is just her really good best friend?

God, I hope so.

I clear my throat, standing so close to her that now I can smell the sweet scent of her. Vanilla maybe? Sweet but also a little earthy, grounding. But more... *more.*

"Hey there, miss."

She turns to me, her face showing nothing but genuine kindness, even to the stranger interrupting her conversation.

And holy shit, I was not prepared.

Wide, perfect eyes. Though, I am not sure I wouldn't find all of her perfect at this point. The brightest green, like blades of tall grass after a night of rain in July, they draw me right in. A little more than a yard between us and I can still see the golden ring that surrounds her pupil. Not to sound too country, but I swear to all it would match my John Deere baler. She's got the most beautifully freckled cheeks, rosy from some sort of blush or whatever it is. The smallest, silver hoop hanging off the side of her alarmingly adorable speckled nose. Her bright red lips are just as I had thought they would be up close, full and impressive.

And the king himself, Johnny fucking Cash, is staring back at me from the front of her t-shirt.

I'd propose right now, honestly.

I sound like a damn lunatic. I know this. But I can't seem to care.

"Hey!" Her smile is wide, showing off straight, white teeth.

Lord have mercy, her voice.

Her voice is deeper than what I had pictured. Not quite raspy but not high pitched like I had assumed. I would listen to her read me the phonebook, that is all I know.

"Are we in your way? I'm so sorry!" She moves to exit her row, trying to go around me to let me in.

Yes, let me in. Please.

She gently places her hand on my bicep to steady herself by the stairs. I reach out and grasp her freckled wrist, stopping her. Her skin is smooth. It takes everything in me to not move my thumb around and trace all of the small brown dots.

"No, no," I rush out. "I'm up a few rows. I just..."

How do I say this without being a creep?

After a moment of quiet contemplation she asks carefully, "Is everything okay?"

She glances up to where I had looked. Ken, who is watching this all with a smile the size of a football field on his annoying face, gives her a small wave.

"Yes," I say, drawing her attention back.

I look down to where my dark tanned hand is still holding her arm. The contrast between us is beautiful. Bright, light skin on her and the dark, weathered skin of mine. She tracks my movement. I slowly remove my grasp, immediately missing the feel of her smoothness beneath my roughness.

"Everything is great. I don't know how to ask this without sounding like a weirdo, so I'm just going to ask it." I see her assumed-friend inch closer.

Totally forgot about him.

"Are you married? Or taken at all?"

The look of surprise on her face is alarming. Did I not ask that right? Was I not respectful enough?

"You want to know if I am married?" she clarifies slowly. Her dark eyebrows are drawn down in clear confusion.

"Yes, ma'am." I nod. "It's just... I noticed you from up there and you're so beautiful that I would have kicked myself all night if I hadn't asked."

Her gorgeous face doesn't change much. I see her bite the inside corner of her bottom lip and that does real funny things to my chest and head.

Focus, dude.

"*You* want to know if *I* am single?" She asks again, emphasizing 'you' and 'I'.

I nod enthusiastically. "Absolutely, I do."

She laughs and I feel like dropping to my damn knees again.

Her green eyes land on my blue ones and she says, "You're kidding right?" Her smile fades a little. "You're not serious." She draws the words out as she narrows her gaze.

"I've never been more serious in my life," I say without a moment of hesitation.

She laughs again, this time a little more and I swear to all I would lay my life down at her sandal-wearing feet to hear that sound for the rest of my life.

She stops laughing, dabbing at her eyes with black polished fingers, before saying, "Oh my gosh, I'm so sorry. That was so rude of me, laughing like that." She straightens, her face falling to a more serious position, and goes on. "I swear I was not laughing at you. Thank you for the compliment. That was very nice of you."

I'm immediately pissed at the tone and phrasing... As though she is trying to be almost diplomatic. Like this is some sort of transaction. As if I could not possibly be sincere.

"You don't believe me." I don't ask it, it's not a question.

"Well..." she scoffs, rolling her spectacular eyes.

"What else would be the reason for me coming down here and being so forward if it weren't true?"

"I mean come on," she says while looking me over and raising her brows. I arch a brow at her and she takes notice that I'm not picking up what she's putting down before continuing. "It could be a bet. Like, with your friends. You could be six beers deep and not thinking clearly. You could have been dared." With each scenario this incredulous woman gives, she ticks them off on her hand.

She shrugs her shoulders, and my irritation grows. Not at her. I don't even know her but still, never at *her*. Who in the fuck made this insanely gorgeous woman doubt that a man could openly and sincerely find her attractive? So much so that she literally does not believe that I am here of my volition?

I hold up my own hand and go over her list. "One beer, an hour ago. My friends did not bet me or dare me. I was sitting up there in my seat, saw you move into your row, felt absolutely drawn to you and I needed— NEED to know if there is any chance in hell of getting your name and number."

"Truly?" Her face scrunches a bit, her nose wrinkling slightly.

I'm trying to continue to not be offended at this point. I don't think I have ever had my intentions questioned so fiercely before.

"Truly." I give one sure nod.

"Wow," she says slowly. "Well, I am sorry then. I shouldn't have been so rude. Thank you, that was really sweet of you."

She takes a moment before responding. I watch her bring her her hands up in front of her chest. That is when I notice it, as her right hand goes to her left. I see her spin a ring around and do the logistics in my head.

Left hand.

Black nails.

Finger next to pinky.

Silver.

Slight scar in the middle of the top of her left hand.

Diamond.

Fuck.

"You're married." I keep my tone even and smile slightly, trying to conceal the absolute devastation I feel.

She snaps her gaze back to mine, reciprocating the same smile, neither of them meeting our eyes.

"Yes, I am married. But seriously, thank you for the compliment. That was really very nice of you."

I nod, not knowing what to say to that.

"Enjoy the rest of your night." Her smile turns more genuine, mine following suit.

"You too, miss." I nod at the man behind her, still not sure if he's her husband. Who would just let a man hit on his wife like that? He's got to be a friend or something.

I take the stairs two at a time as I ascend them to go sit back down. Before I know it though, I am walking past my row and to the hallway. I ignore Ken's hackling on my way.

I am going to go buy her a drink. She had a purple White Claw sitting by her feet. Buying her a drink will not hurt a damn thing. Right?

Right.

Kris

I turn, looking forward again, before I can even be tempted to watch *him* walk away.

"What the fuck was that?" Bryce asks.

"Well, you were here, so you saw exactly what it was," I say dismissively.

I'm sure he is back up with his friend now. He has to be around two inches over six feet, built like a fucking linebacker, and incredibly hot. And *he* had come down here to see if *I* am single? Me? He is all thick thighs under those well-fitted jeans. Broad shoulders that had his t-shirt stretched nicely across his chest. And that quick touch of his upper arm told me all I needed to know about what is certainly not lacking there. Not a chance that was all real. *Me?* The girl with hips that are "meant for birthing." The woman with already sagging boobs and pale skin that does not tan. A belly that I couldn't hide even if I tried. Chins; plural. Yeah, right.

I scoff out loud at the ridiculousness.

I definitely did not have "hot man hits on me" on my Eric Church Bingo card. I'm sure my brother is eating this shit up. He is standing silently beside me. I bet his arms are crossed and he's probably wearing that permanent scowl of his on his adorable face like some mute

Northern mob boss. I avoid looking over to confirm any of that, not wanting to start a discussion.

Bryce and I sit back down in our seats, there is about another forty minutes until the opener will probably start. Getting here early was the right move though. Shit was packed by the time we showed up. I cannot imagine how congested it is now out in the halls.

Gosh, did that feel nice though. Once I understood that he was serious and *hopefully* not joking around, that is. To be told I am beautiful by a stranger is just... He had no obligation to say or think that. But he did anyway. It is shocking.

"As your twin," Bryce starts from beside me, his green eyes glaring at me. "The fact that he told you how pretty you are, and you didn't believe him is concerning. Because if you don't think you're pretty, then how unfortunate is that for me? We look the same, Kris."

I smack his arm and roll my eyes.

"If I had a penis, I would probably think I am hot shit. Don't get your feelings hurt buddy."

Really though, for not being identical twins we look quite similar. Same shade of thick auburn hair. Same rounded out hairline. Same dark eyebrows, his bushier than mine when I remember to tweeze. Same bright green eyes, except Bryce doesn't have the golden ring I was blessed with. His build is different in the sense that he looks like the standard "attractive" male, or so I have been told by every girl I have ever been friends with. Broad shoulders, trim waist, long legs. Bryce's tan-less skin works for him.

If I were a size eight instead of eighteen and a hundred pounds skinnier, with shoulders that weren't as wide as my dads, I'd be the "classical" pretty. To the majority at least. That is what I have been told a time or two.

I like *me* though. I like how my hips crease. I like that my stomach is soft to the touch, although I wouldn't complain if there was not so much of it. I would also not be pissed if I could catch a nice tan but that just is what it is. I like who I am inside as well, I think that helps a lot.

Bryce and I settle into comfortable conversation. We catch up on his new girlfriend, Sherry, that he thinks is "the one". Which, for Bryce, is entirely too common of a phenomenon. I tell him about the new job I just got and how it's remote so I can work from wherever. He tells me that means I can visit mom and dad more. And then we both laugh at that joke.

I don't even think about *him*. Well, not for longer than a few seconds at a time. And I never let myself look up to where his friend was at. Except that one time that I had to crack my neck... But that was necessary.

Convincing.

"Oh shit," Bryce whispers from beside me.

I turn to him to ask what. Before I get it out, though, there is a dewy White Claw being put in front of my face.

"I got you a drink."

Just one conversation and I think I might know that voice anywhere.

"It's just a drink, before you panic. Nothing with strings or proposals. And I even had the bartender leave it closed so you wouldn't be nervous that I might have done something to it."

He had the bartender...

"What?"

He says it so matter of fact that I can't help but to openly gape at him. The way his cheeks blush a little melts my heart. I drag my eyes from his face as I stand up, trailing down his long, tan, muscular arm. I look at his large hand, nearly taking up all of the can, before I reach out and take it from him.

"If you let me know when you need another drink, I'll go up with you and get your next one," I say as I crack the top. "Thank you for this."

We stay put, me in front of him and him on the stairs with one booted foot on the step above him, one hand braced on that knee. My hands encompass my new drink as I rub the condensation around with my thumbs. His army green Tractor Supply shirt hugs his biceps just enough to allow me to take quick notice of them. Those and the black ink just under the hem of one of his sleeves. It looks like wings. Angel maybe? Possibly bird wings? They are black and gray and look as if they wrap the entire way around.

Married.

Married married married.

And unhappy.

Doesn't matter. Married.

I tell the imaginary devil and angel in my ears to shut the hell up.

I smile at him and take a drink, directing my eyes to the bridge of the can as I do.

When I look back up, his gaze is still on me.

"Was there... anything else? Is there something on my face or something?"

He shakes his head like he was lost in thought.

"No, nothing like that. Your face is perfect."

I would be unable to hide the blush that rushes to my cheeks even if I tried.

"I'm just... I'm honestly and unnecessarily bothered by how convinced you were that I was kidding or put up to it. The whole me coming down here to talk to you thing."

I look down, embarrassed. Not by him or what he said but by me and my insecurities.

"I'm sorry. I didn't mean to bother you by that," I say quietly.

He squats down slightly, putting himself at my eye level, forcing me to look AT him. I hear Bryce clear his throat and move just a little closer to my back, but I cannot be bothered to pay attention to him right now.

"It isn't you that has me bothered. It's whatever or whomever in your life that has made you feel unworthy of being told you're incredible. You seem genuinely kind, even just from the small interaction we have had. So, for someone to have made you think that a stranger couldn't possibly mean it when they tell you that you are beautiful..." He shakes his head. "I've watched you." His eyes go wide before he rushes out, "Not in a creepy way! Though, maybe it kind of was. It's just... The second you walked into this arena, my eyes were drawn to you. I couldn't look away. I saw you and your...?" He looks around me slightly.

Bryce reaches around me and holds out his right hand. "Bryce, her *brother*," he says proudly and almost pointedly.

They shake hands and *he* smiles widely before he goes on. "I saw you and your brother singing to the songs they've been playing over the speakers. I watched you dance around and smile and laugh and move out of people's way and even offer some of them help to figure out which row they were supposed to go to. And you just seem so cool and nice and now I definitely sound like a creep but I swear it wasn't like a weird watching kind of thing."

I laugh softly as I watch him spiral a bit.

"I just wanted to meet you and I have so now I'll go but please know; you're beautiful and I mean that from the bottom of my heart, miss."

Before I can say a word, he nods his head at me and Bryce and walks up the stairs to his seat. This time, I do not stop myself from watching.

"Holy shit," I breathe out.

"Obviously we won't be mentioning this to Michael." My brother's tone carrying every ounce of his annoyance with my husband in the way he says his name.

I roll my eyes at the mention of Michael. The sound of his name is like a cold bucket of water being tossed on to my head.

"Obviously."

Carter

"I swear to all, Kenny. She's the fucking one."

"Well, she can't be the one because she's married, dumb ass."

I glare at my best friend as the opener, some dude with skinny jeans and a white cut off t-shirt, takes the stage and begins his first song.

"Just my fucking luck, too. But I'm serious, brother. She's the one."

I cannot explain it. The pull— the drift I feel to this stranger. My eyes don't stray for long from the kind brunette standing by her brother for long throughout the entire concert.

Brother, fuck yes.

Married. Shit.

I watch her as she bounces around and claps her hands in time with the beat. She's incredible.

Ken pats my shoulder and speaks loudly over the music. "The one you can't have., Car."

I punch him in the arm, and he laughs.

Prick.

"I'll be right back." Before Ken can argue or stop me, I am rushing down the stairs as Eric Church sings his last encore of the night.

I'm standing, nearly frozen to the spot, next to *her* again. I did not think this far ahead. Sure, I had the entire concert to think of something to say, but all I could work up was something about how much I liked talking to her and being in her space. Not good enough.

Like she can feel me get closer, she turns her green eyes to me and waits, her lips parting slightly.

I yell over the music, her brother now watching and listening too. "Listen. This is not something I do. You can ask my buddy if you want. I don't come out strong like this. But... Well... And then I saw you. This is crazy and I know that. And I know you're married, and this is morally problematic and not cool at all, but I just feel this like, insane connection to you and I think I would kick myself in the ass for the rest of my life if I didn't come down here one more time." My heart is racing a million miles a minute. The bass from the music is making my face feel like it's vibrating. That is what this woman is doing to my heart too, so it's all I can do to try to make sense as I continue to holler at her. "If your situation ever changes and you find yourself available again, I just need you to know that wherever I am, come find me. Wherever you are, I want to be there. Because, and again, I *know* this sounds insane and completely unhinged, but I think you might be it for me." I watch the surprise roll over her face. I do not blame her. I have been feeling the same wave of shock all night.

She is quiet for a moment and then laughs and waves her hand in the air. "Yeah, okay. Sure." Her laugh is a bitter one and I can taste the doubt coming from her. And still, I will not fault her for that.

This whole thing is fucking ludicrous.

"Carter Barker. Ragan, Nebraska. Twenty-seven." I say it slowly and clearly, wildly confident for the situation.

She turns her shocked face to her brother. His smile is small, but it has me curious to know what he is thinking. She turns back to me, and her expression gives nothing away.

"I hope that one day you won't doubt when someone tells you you're beautiful."

I don't give her a chance to laugh me off or question anything again. I turn on my heel and exit the arena. As I wait for Ken by my pickup, I can't help but smile.

She is the fucking one. I do not know her name or where she is from, but she is it for me. Even if I never get the chance to see her again, I will never be sorry for a single thing I said to that insanely wonderful woman tonight.

I smile and start thinking about her all over again.

I did not know feeling like this was even possible for me.

"And then I saw you," I whisper at the thought of *her.*

Chapter One

Remember When

Five Years Later, August 2023

Kris

"Well, that's it I guess."

I run a hand through my freshly cut lob. My "divorce-cut" as my hairdresser called it last week sits just under my collarbone in a straight style and is the most beautiful shade of espresso with pieces of caramel layered throughout.

Makes me think of all of the chocolate I want to eat my weight in right now.

I take one last look around our— *my* apartment. Or rather, my *old* apartment.

"It was real, it was fun. Can't say it's been real fun though." My joke falls flat to the empty space, bouncing unenthusiastically off the bare white walls.

It's just me standing here in the open doorway. The cooling breeze at my back ruffles my dingy black t-shirt and causes goosebumps to pebble my exposed arms. It's eighty-six-degrees today here in Fargo, North Dakota, so my arms lose the bumps as quickly as they came. It has been only me in this apartment for months now. Longer than that, really. Even before Michael and I separated in January and he moved out, I was alone here.

"You coming?"

I pivot to look at my brother waiting in the driveway. Bryce is leaning against the side of his black Toyota pickup, his brown t-shirt covered in spots of dust from moving boxes and furniture all day.

"Yeah, I'm coming. Hang on."

I turn to look at what *was* my life one final time. The breath I take feels lighter than I thought it would. There are no tears lining my eyes, Lord knows this place has seen plenty of those from me in the last five years. I smile sadly, the memories aren't all bad. I recall the day Michael and I moved in here seven years ago. The laughs we shared while we sat on lawn chairs in the living room, our couch having not arrived for two more weeks. We watched "Without a Paddle" on Michael's laptop that sat on top of two boxes that housed our DVD's. Everything was so simple then. Life, us, me.

Until it wasn't.

I place the key in the gray lockbox that hangs from the brass door handle after shutting the door.

Bryce meets me at the driver's side door of my dark blue Camry.

"Officially closing that chapter," I say as I lean one hip on my car, running my hands down my black leggings.

"I was thinking," Bryce starts.

"That's never a good thing."

He rolls his eyes at my joke but continues on. "You remember that concert we went to in South Dakota a few years ago?"

"Of course."

"Do you remember that guy that talked to you a few times? The one that bought you a drink?"

How could I forget?

"Yes, Bryce." My patience is thin today and I just want to go to Bryce's house and relax after this long week. Between fielding calls from our loudly concerned parents, mainly our overbearing but well-intentioned mother, and still working on a huge project at work and packing and moving and trying to keep myself put together... I'm just simply beat. "What about it?"

"Don't get snippy with me." Bryce boops my nose with his finger and I imagine how nice it would feel to unleash my pent-up frustration onto my annoying twin. "Do you remember what he said that night before he left?"

"No."

Liar.

I could never forget *him*. The timber of his rough voice. The way his blue eyes shined under all of the arena lights like stars. How he smelled like chewing tobacco and beer and also minty gum but in like, a hot cowboy kind of way. I recall how cute he was in a baseball cap and wanting to see how dark and thick his hair was underneath.

Bryce sees through my lie of course but instead of calling me out on it he says, "Carter Barker. Nebraska. Twenty-"

"Seven," I say impatiently, tapping my foot on the driveway.

What is the point of this conversation? Why does Bryce need to bring this up right now as I close the page on a huge chapter of my life? Our divorce papers aren't even cold yet, the ink might not even be dry.

More lies.

"He's thirty-three now." Bryce winks, ignoring the steam coming out of my ears.

"Yes, Bryce. That's how aging and time passing works. Can we go?"

He shakes his head, his shaggy dark brown hair falling in front of his eyes in the process.

"Ugh. I'm tired, okay? This is dumb. I'm sure he's married, happily, to some lucky woman with two Nebraskan babies and a dog. Or four." I roll my eyes and put on my brown tortoise shell sunglasses as I move to open my car door.

"I'll see you at your hou-"

I'm stopped by a hand on my shoulder.

"It's okay to be okay by now, Kris."

I laugh coldly and shrug Bryce off, not wanting to get into all of this. Not because it hurts... but because it *doesn't*.

It should. Leaving this place. Moving in with my brother. Not speaking to Michael anymore. Being divorced at twenty-seven-years-old. I should be sad. I should *feel* something about all of this shit, but I simply do not. All I feel is exhaustion from the packing and cleaning and moving. And I feel relief that it's all finally over. And annoyance towards my nosy twin.

What does that say about me? Am I broken like Michael always thought? So damaged that I can't even grieve the life I thought I would have properly?

Like he read my mind, Bryce says, "Everyone grieves things the way they need to. Just because you aren't sobbing on the floor of a bathroom and drinking yourself to sleep-"

"How do you know I'm not?" I interrupt, raising my brows.

I'm not.

"You're not." He levels me with an unamused glare. "If you were that would be perfectly fine though. Anyways. You're not damaged or fucked up. Where you are in all of this is fine, sis."

Bryce lets me go when I do not do anything other than tell him I *am* fine. As I follow him to the home he shares with his fiancé, Sherry, I turn up my radio. Drowning out, or getting out, my thoughts with music has always been something I find solace in. Today is no different while Breaking Benjamin's "Breath" blares through my speakers. My open window serves as an exit for the bad feelings I am belting out along with the song.

After getting settled into the guest room at "Casa Atwater" as Sherry calls it, I toss my toothbrush and shampoo into the bathroom that is attached to "my" room. It's not hard feeling at home here. I've put small things away and helped Sherry get the table set for supper. Bryce couldn't even manage one night of reprieve before diving into my mildly unstable life.

"Honey, give her a break. She's fine." Sherry turns her gaze to me, her hazel eyes meeting mine, "You stay for however long you want to, Krissy. You're welcome here. Always."

And she means it too. That is Sherry. Kind, beautiful inside and out, generous. All five feet, three inches of her is saintly. The height and bounce of her bright salon-blonde hair matches perfectly with the insanely lovely lilt of her southern Georgia accent. She is every bit a lady and my brother could not do better if he tried.

I glare at Bryce before smiling at Sherry. "Thank *you*, Sher. I appreciate your hospitality. If only *someone else* could chill out and leave me be for one single evening. You're spoiling this delicious peach cobbler Sherry made, Bryce. Back. Off." I smile at him as he rolls his eyes.

"Obviously you can stay here. That's not what I'm saying. I'm just saying that you work remotely. You can go wherever you want. Do whatever you want. Be whoever you want. Be WITH whomever you want." His pointed gaze grates on my last nerve as I entertain the idea of stabbing him with his own fork.

He isn't wrong, he is just annoying. I can do and go wherever I wish right now. My job is incredible that way. I work for a web design company. It's a small company but incredibly successful with clients like major grocery stores and chain restaurants. I can work from anywhere.

"You could go to fucking Nebraska if you wanted."

I do not miss the way he says Nebraska. What is his deal with this all of a sudden?

I point my cobbler covered spoon at my twin. "Let. Me. Be. Bryce. Give me one fucking night, at least."

His shoulders relax, his chest expands before he lets out a sigh. "I just want you to be happy, Kris. That's all."

I know he does. He means well. He watched me live unhappily for years.

"This cobbler is making me happy at the moment so please, let that be enough for now. Okay?"

"Yeah, okay. Sorry." He smiles at me before turning his attention to Sherry and for the first time all evening, I finally have a minute to breathe.

Nebraska and a studly man from somewhere called "Ragan" don't reenter my thoughts for two more bites of dessert. And by the time I lay down for bed, Carter Barker is *definitely* not walking his fine ass through my dreams.

Chapter Two

Cowboy Take Me Away

Kris

Cohabitating with my twin brother and his bubbly fiancé for the last two weeks has been as easy as breathing. Seriously. I love Sherry. She is a second-grade teacher and is always bringing home hilarious stories about the glue-eaters. Bryce works as a manager of a grocery store and always comes home grumbling about something that annoyed him; which is everything. He lightens up the second Sherry gives him a hug though. It is grossly wonderful. I would be lying if I said I do not envy what they have. They seem to love each other so easily. Is that what it is supposed to be like? *Easy?*

As I read the last page of the book I started two days ago, I get swept away in this wave of emotion that I cannot quite place.

"And for the first time in years, I feel like things are going to turn out the way they were always meant to be."

If He Had Been With Me has me wrecked. Emotionally, in every way possible. The whole book felt like one big, bad car accident that I couldn't look away from and then BOOM; fucked me up. I am unwell.

And I am loving every second of it.

Masochist.

I am also inspired. Life is short. It is unexpected and quick and painful but beautiful, and what am I doing with it if I allow myself to not just go for what I think I might want? What a disservice am I doing to myself by hindering my desires and wants and needs? I feel jumpy and impulsive. Like I want to go buy a coffee and a new comforter for a bed that is in a storage unit. I feel like I want to hurl myself out of an airplane— a moving one! Or stand on the front of a boat with my arms spread open and my eyes closed while singing "My Heart Will Go On." I feel... like I want to *live*. You get one shot. One life. One opportunity.

Eminem makes complete sense.

"I'm going to Nebraska."

Sherry stops drying the white plate in her hands and looks up at me from her spot in their bright kitchen. Bryce pauses mid-step on his way to the fridge, leftover taco fixings in hand. They both look at me for a moment as though I have sprouted wings and am now levitating off their gray couch three yards from them. My hair is up in a neon pink claw clip, and I've worn the same yellow Zach Bryan t-shirt for the last two days. My sparkly black glasses are resting halfway down my nose, and I know the tears I just cried from this damn book are still reflecting light off my cheeks. I look depressed, unbathed, and maybe slightly insane; I swear I *am* fine though.

Mostly.

I watch them watching me before they both smile and turn to each other and high-five.

"What are you guys doing?"

I am utterly confused. Perhaps they didn't hear me?

"I said-"

"We heard you," they say in unison, nodding their heads and smiling still.

"Then why are you high-fiving? Do you hate me being here that much?"

I feel more tears line my eyes and try to hold them at bay. That book has seriously messed with my already dicey emotions.

Bryce and Sherry rush to the living room, both coming down on the couch on either side of me. Bryce envelopes me in a hug, his long arms holding tight. I push my tears down and choke on the sob trying to escape. I am typically not emotional like this. But fertility issues, a shitty marriage, a divorce, moving in with your brother, and then a really devastating book will fuck a girl up.

"We love you being here," Sherry says as she wraps her golden bronzed arms around my brothers, hugging me from the other side. "We just hate knowing you're sad. We don't know how to help. We have just been-"

"Waiting for you to find something inside of yourself that tells you to do more. To be more. Because-"

"You're so wonderful and so beautiful and so smart and you could be so, so, so-"

"Happy! If you would just let yourself be happy."

I look from side to side, my blonde almost-sister-in-law smiling so wide I think I can see her molars. My twin brother looking at me like he knows every thought I have had in the last two weeks.

"I thought we were the twins? That was really freaky, the whole finishing each other's sentence's thing you two just did there."

The three of us laugh. Neither Bryce nor Sherry lighten their hold on me.

Bryce presses his forehead to my temple.

After a minute of quiet, soaking in the love my two favorite people in the world are pouring into me, Bryce speaks up. "Nebraska, eh? Surely not for a very handsome, tall, swaggering mystery guy, right?"

I shove at him lightly but say nothing.

"Let's check flights!" Sherry pops up from the couch. "I'll grab my computer!"

Bryce scoots over a few inches, releasing me from his hug.

"What if he is married? Or what if I can't find him? Or what if he *was* smashed out of his mind and he doesn't remember me at all?" My voice is barely above a whisper.

I pull at a loose string on my black leggings while I wait for Bryce to say something. When he doesn't, I finally look up and over at him.

"Then so what?"

My eyes widen.

"So what if he doesn't remember or doesn't care or he is married? You'll have *done* something Kris. When was the last time you did something for you and only you? Not me. Not Sherry. Not mom or dad. Not Michael. For *you* and only *you*. When was the last time you made *you* your priority?"

I sit back, crossing my legs underneath me and pulling my shirt out from where it catches in my little belly rolls. I continue to pull at the loose string on my pants while I think over what Bryce just said. He remains quiet, knowing he is certainly not wrong, while scrolling Facebook on his phone. Sherry springs back in from their office with her rose gold laptop and starts looking up flights, as though I won't be just driving down there. It cannot be THAT far.

So, I'm left here. In this emotional limbo, questioning myself and everything I am.

When WAS the last time I focused on me? On my wants?

While we were growing up I focused on the twin thing, our bond and staying together and growing up in a way that was conducive to a healthy relationship with Bryce and my parents. I too often saw families falling apart, and I refused to be one of them. After school I focused on a career that would put me somewhere that I could be anywhere. I wanted to be readily available for my parents as they aged, and my brother as we grew older. I met Michael and we fell in love. My career was already something that was no bother for him and his needs, so it was just a matter of staying pliant. Of being what he needed, when he needed it. So, I did that. I molded and bended, and did what I felt I had to do to have a happy marriage. Until my body told us both to fuck off, that is. After enduring years of excruciating pain, both mentally and physically, while trying to conceive, we found out that I could not have kids. I knew it was only a matter of time until Michael realized I could not be what he needed; the mother of his children. And while that fact was a crushing blow to me and my mental health, no one took it harder than the man I had married. It was like he had realized I was broken or something. So, I tried what I could to be something more, something different, for him and clearly that failed. I lost a lot of myself in the process. And now here I am.

Divorced and not even thirty. And for the first time I am ready to do something for myself. To find what I want and go after it.

"-into Lincoln on the-"

"Start over," I say, interrupting Sherry. "Sorry. I honestly zoned out. I'm here now though, start over."

She winks at me, not upset by my wandering mind or the interruption.

A little while later and a bummed-about-no-flying Sherry, Bryce finds me an Airbnb close to Ragan, Nebraska. Before I know it, I am packed, again, and ready.

"Ready" being used incredibly loosely here.

The weather in Nebraska is wildly similar to North Dakota. Warmer but nice. The hustle and bustle of the interstates and highways on the way down here was a lot. But the drive took just over nine hours so all in all, I won't complain. Much.

I'm staying in a town called Alma and the maps app on my phone says Ragan is about twenty minutes away. I passed a sign for it on my way down here, so at least I know it's real.

My legs feel tired, but my body is restless. Before I spin out of control, I decide to unpack all of my clothes into the little cabin I am renting for the foreseeable future. My thoughts wander to Carter and then the drive here and the possibilities that go along with this entire situation. I did not have the balls to look up his information beyond the town he is in, so detective-wannabe Sherry gathered the info I needed for a successful mission.

She watches too many investigative TV shows.

This little cabin is a lovely single-wide trailer. It has two-bedrooms and a bathroom. The very on-brand nautical theme throughout is definitely upping my mood and calming my anxious brain. I love a cliché. After I settle my things in my room and park myself onto the queen-sized bed in here, I take in some details, grounding myself. The white comforter is airy, and the walls are a soft, buttery blue color. Seashells and little cartoon fish are sprinkled throughout on walls and light-colored dressers and shelves.

It is cute and quaint and charming. And with a working air conditioner, I am more than content.

I prop my phone up on the light brown nightstand, letting it rest against the white alarm clock, waiting for my mom to pick up my FaceTime call.

I don't have to wait long.

"Honey!" Mom's high pitched voice comes out of the phone loudly.

I laugh a little. It's the same greeting every time. Penny Atwater has very little chill. Born and raised in Fargo, she is every bit a Northerner. Her dark, straight hair is pulled back into a beige scrunchy. Her green eyes, identical to Bryce's, squint as she gets a good look at me.

"You made it to your hotel then, honey? It looks cute! Take me on a tour!"

"I just sat down, I'll call you again tomorrow and show you around." I ignore her pout. I also do not correct the fact that she called this cabin a hotel and ask, "What's dad up to?"

"Oh, he's out getting some groceries, dear. He'll be bummed he missed you."

My dad does the shopping. He learned early on that my mom's attention span is far too small for an "appropriate" grocery haul.

"That's okay, I'll call later. I was just calling to tell you I got to my place. I'm going to run now though. Have dad hug you for me."

"No problem, honey. Get some rest. You look a little tired. Love ya!"

I reign in the urge to roll my eyes slightly. "Love you too, mom."

We blow each other a couple of kisses like we always do before hanging up.

I love my mom.

In small doses.

I intentionally had only Bryce help me move because I knew she would be a bit of a wreck and my nerves could not have handled that. She means well, always. Bryce gets that from her. But she is batty in the very best way. Her feelings run a little rampant sometimes, especially about her kids and if their lives are maybe a little more strenuous than usual. Quick phone calls and a lot of our boundaries are the key to our survival.

Alright, Kris. You've got this. Let's go find that cowboy.

I push up off the bed with my hands on my knees and take a deep steadying breath. It *is* fine. It will *stay* fine. I could— maybe— *might* be fine.

Chapter Three

Livin' On a Prayer

Carter

This heat is on my damn nerves. I'm over it. I miss the cold and football season.

It's not that it is even THAT hot outside today, I know. Eighties are nothing, but damn, I am ready for fall. I am ready for the humidity to hit the curb and the stickiness of being outside to be over.

I kick the heel of my boot on the concrete step, knocking chunks of dirt off it before switching to the other foot and repeating the process. I hear the sound of a car pulling up the long driveway. Unable to see who it is around the large pine trees that line my property I assume it's Ken, or maybe Sadie and Cameron. I finish kicking off my boots and move through my front door, leaving it open so I can see out the screen door.

Either Ken or Sadie and Cameron, they will just let themselves in.

As I wash my hands at the kitchen sink, the dirt-stained water running down the sides of white porcelain, I hear a car door close. Soft, slow footsteps come across the porch. The knock on the screen door catches me off guard.

No one knocks around here.

Grabbing a worn, once-was-white towel off the counter, I dry my hands as I round the corner from the kitchen to the front door.

"Come on i-"

There's no damn way.

"Hi."

Move.

Do something.

Speak, man!

Idiot.

"Um... I don't mean to intrude. I was just... Well, you know, I don't really know what I'm doing and if I'm being honest that— feeling like I don't know what is happening or what to do, it is not something that is very familiar to me. And now I'm rambling, but I drove in today and went to the house I'm staying at and it just felt so weird to have your potential address on a piece of paper in my purse and just have it like, sitting there, waiting, and I couldn't just come all the way down here and just not like, find you and I'm sorry if this is so way too late or too insane or you probably definitely think I'm a crazy person for just like, hunting you down like thi-"

The long step I took towards *her* stops her incredibly attractive rambling, her train of thought dying on her tongue.

I watch her throat bob as I scan her from head to toe.

How did she get more beautiful?

The same seemingly thick hair. Now, though, it's darker and shorter and straight with little bends in it. It has streaks of bright pieces, like someone placed small bits of sunlight throughout. Her green eyes are behind a pair of sparkling black framed glasses. A silver hoop is in her cute nose still. Her lips are not painted red like they were the first and only time I have seen her, but the natural pink color has my heart nearly coming out of my chest. From her loose gray t-shirt to her tight black leggings and her black sandals, I can see nearly every hip and dip and curve.

She's here.

"How-" I cut myself off not knowing what the fuck to say.

She points her thumb to the little blue car sitting in front of my house. "I can go-"

"No!" I all but shout, as I just barely hold myself back from lunging at her.

She lets out a soft laugh and her small smile nearly takes me down to my fucking knees.

"No, sorry. No. Don't go. Come in, please." I take one more step, finally getting to the door and opening it. She does not move to come in, instead she bites the inside of her cheek and pulls at a ring that sits on her right hand.

"I don't honestly know what I'm doing." She says it so quietly I almost don't hear her.

She's far enough from the door that there is room for me to slip out onto the porch. It snicks shut behind me as I step between it and the woman of my actual dreams. I try to act casual, leaning my back against it. I am feeling anything but casual right now.

"I just realized I don't even know your name." I hold out my right hand, "I'm Carter." I flash her a smile, making it a little extra big to hopefully lighten the mood.

She pauses for a few seconds before placing her incredibly soft hand in to mine. If I did not already know how completely fucked I am, I would now. She's going to have to pry her perfect hand from mine if she ever wants it back.

"Kris. Kris Atwater." I watch her as she lets out a deep breath.

Neither of us move to end our handshake.

"It's very nice to meet you, Kris Atwater." I don't lessen my smile, hoping to convey how nice it really is. "Again."

Her smile grows and good lord, if I did not think she would run away I would drop to one knee and propose right now for that fucking smile.

Is that wildly insane? Absolutely. But here I am.

"Come inside?" I ask again. "I've got some beer, water. Juice pouches."

She laughs again, this one a little less hidden beneath nerves.

"Okay."

Fuck yes.

It takes everything in me to not fist pump into the air above my head like Judd Nelson in *The Breakfast Club*. Though, Simple Minds "Don't You (Forget About Me)" would be incredibly fitting in this moment.

"Your house is lovely," Kris says.

Her voice is like my favorite song. I could listen to it on repeat day in and day out.

"How long have you lived here?"

"A little over five years. It's a part of the farm that surrounds it. So, when things started breaking down for the previous owners, them wanting to sell and move, this place came up and I knew it was where I wanted to be. I worked for the farmer then, driving truck and whatever else they needed. Been here since."

I turn to her, a beer in each hand, to find her smiling at me from where she is sitting at my dining room table.

Looking like she belongs here.

"Now I'm rambling, huh?"

Her laugh fills my ears. It invades my heart, my soul, my home.

I sit down opposite her at my small, old, square table. The wood creaks as I lean back and bring my beer to my lips.

"So..." I say slowly.

Kris takes a drink of her beer and I find myself feeling jealous of the bottle.

"So..." she repeats at the same pace.

"You drove in today, then? I don't even know where you live. Or lived?"

"Fargo," she nods. "Yeah, I got here a couple hours ago. It was like, a nine-hour drive, I think. The cabin I'm staying at is cute. I went there first."

"Oh? Where's that at? Close? Good neighborhood?"

I swear to all, if she is in one of the shittier towns around here, I will drive there myself and cancel her reservation. I'll pay whatever damn fee necessary.

"It's actually not far. Like, twenty minutes from here. Alma. By some lake."

Thank you, God.

"Great. That's great." I take another drink.

Be chill.

My phone buzzes from my pocket, we both look down towards it. When I pull it out, I see it is Sadie and I internally swear at her bad timing. Cameron is not with me until tomorrow afternoon. But... the mother of my child is calling, and I cannot ignore her.

"I'm sorry," I say, gesturing to my phone and rising from my chair.

"No, no. Don't be. Go ahead, I'm fine."

"I'll be just a minute." I get up and walk to the living room a few yards away. "Hey, what's up?"

"Hey Cars! Listen, I know it's your weekend with Cameron, but I just got tickets to this Disney on Ice thing in Omaha. I want to take Cameron to it, but I want to make a whole weekend of it. Well, Lance wants to make it this whole thing. Can we switch weekends? I'm so sorry it's so short-"

Awesome timing Sadie.

"No, yeah! That's fine. He'll love that!" I try to keep my cool. It's not unlike us to go along with each other's requests when it comes to Cameron. Co-parenting with Sadie has been a dream the last two years.

"Oh gosh, thanks Cars! I really appreciate it!"

"No problem. Give him a kiss for me, yeah?"

"You bet! Bye!"

I round the corner back into the kitchen, tucking my phone into my front pocket. Kris doesn't notice so I take a second to catalog this moment.

Her new-to-me hair. The way it shines under my warm lighting. I notice the way she rubs the condensation on her beer bottle with her thumb. The way she chews on her bottom lip while she surveys my old kitchen. Her foot, in sandals again, taps on the floor to some mysterious beat that must be sounding off in her beautiful head.

I clear my throat and finish my walk to the table. Our eyes connect and we both smile slightly. There is this odd feeling that is present, obviously. But I'm hoping she is feeling it the same way I am. Because it's not just a strangeness. There is also a rightness settling into this room.

"You eat dinner yet, Kris Atwater?" I can't stop the smile from plastering itself to my face.

As she shakes her head no, I send up every "thank you" and "please don't let me fuck this up" I can manage to the Big Man upstairs.

Chapter Four

Chicken Fried

Kris

I did it. I drove my happy ass to the address Sherry gave me, sent her a pin to my location just in case Carter turns out to be a serial killer with good hair, and walked right up to his door and knocked.

And I was not disappointed in the slightest. He is more handsome than I remember. His hair is still the same warm black that peaked out under his hat five years ago. His eyes are the color of blue sapphires. His dark brows frame them perfectly, with the most beautiful eyelashes. The short black scruff, that he did not have last time, runs along his jaw and above his perfectly shaped lips. It is speckled with bright white throughout, and I can't help but want to run my hands thro-

Get a grip. He just found out what your own name is.

I was mildly shocked by how picturesque his home is, as I pulled in. It's old but in incredible shape. I had to drive on about three miles of gravel from the highway, and then another half a mile or so from that road to his house. I parked on the concrete slab at the end of his rocky driveway. The whole lot is surrounded by large, blue-green pine trees. A home surrounded by those is not anything unusual to me. That is pretty standard in North Dakota to block the snow or wind or any other kind of inclement weather from hitting your house straight on. There's a thin, old sidewalk that led me from the concrete pad in front of his attached three car garage to his front porch. The large porch alone had me dying to see the rest of his house. It's beautiful. White, worn, and loved. He has an old, weathered dark brown swing hanging from the ceiling on one side of the white door. On the other side of the porch is a short rectangular table surrounded by a loveseat and three chairs. Carter even has a ceiling fan above that setup. Strings of lights line the entire thing, the kind with the large bulbs. There are empty flower beds that line the front of the porch, and on my way up the first time I noticed a small red tricycle sitting near one on the far side of the house. I pushed the whole front of the house to the back of my brain as I knocked on his white screen door, though. I did not get a tour of the inside once we moved our meeting there but from what I did see, it is gorgeous. Bright gray walls throughout, black stainless appliances in his large, adjoined kitchen and dining room. Windows everywhere that let in the most beautiful natural light that bounces off of every surface, with beautiful sage green curtains hanging from the ceiling to the bottom of the frames. Clean. It is all so clean. When Carter took his phone call, I didn't even have the wherewithal to move from my spot and look around or scope anything else out.

Now, as we walk to the driveway, I cannot help but feel overwhelmed again by this entire situation.

I just drove nine hours to a random town in a state I have never even been to. All so that I could knock on a stranger's door in the hopes of, what? A romance? A conversation? A beer? A one-night stand?

Before I could spiral any further, I feel Carter's large hand on my lower back and look to where he is standing beside me.

He gestures to a black Chevy pickup parked in the space next to my car. "We can take this. Come on."

I smile and nod and allow him to lead me to his truck. He walks me to the passenger side and opens the door for me.

"Thank you," I say as I climb up.

He pauses at the door, not closing it, and I look over and down at where he is standing. His blue eyes are locked onto mine now and his gaze is unwavering. I think in any other situation I might find this exchange odd... But for some reason, Carter staring at me with the corners of his lips lifting slightly and little wrinkles near the edges of his eyes, I do not seem to mind at all.

"You okay?" I ask carefully.

His face gives nothing away. I cannot tell what he is thinking or feeling or what he is doing right now.

"Carter?"

It's as if his name from my mouth awoke him. Like he was not in his own head for a moment. I watch as his eyes come back to life, to this minute.

"I'm great."

And I believe him. I don't know this man, clearly, or how he operates or who he is as a person. But I believe him right now.

"I'm so glad you're here, Kris."

I smile and feel my cheeks blush. "Me too, Carter."

Carter said that I showed up on the perfect day. For chicken fried steak at Triple S's, that is.

He was not wrong. The restaurant/bar is in the town over; Wilcox. Being from the northern Midwest I am no stranger to small towns. Wilcox is charming. Small enough for one stoplight but big enough for a school. Consolidated with a neighboring town, but it is still a feat.

The ten-minute drive over was filled with aimless chatter. Carter asked me about very easy topics. The weather in North Dakota; similar to here. The construction I had to have hit on the way down; I wanted to claw my eyes out. If I had any pets; no, I don't really like dogs or cats. Not once did he venture into any sort of heavier topics, and I am so grateful to him for that. The food was incredible, and the beers flowed nicely. The whole is-this-a-first-date experience went smoothly.

Now though, as we drive back to Carter's home and the sun finishes its descent, I cannot help the urge to just unload all of my truth onto this handsome man sitting next to me. It's as though my soul wants to be opened up to his.

"I'm divorced."

I cringe at my lacking grace. Carter doesn't, though. The man does not even flinch at my abrupt confession.

"I was hoping that was the case. Even if that makes me an asshole," he says as he smiles and looks over at me briefly.

I focus on the horizon. The sky here is far more colorful than back home. Tonight's sunset is dozens of different shades of orange. Bright, burnt, blood... They all blend and melt together to create this beautifully soft view.

I clear my throat. "We got divorced officially in March. Separated in January. Before that we had both kind of checked out a while ago. Um, he's in Montana now, I think. No hard feelings."

No feelings at all, really.

Carter looks at me again as he flicks his blinker on. His face is so calm and serious as he says, "I'm sorry about your marriage. I can't imagine that it was an easy decision."

I feel a little surprised by his sincerity.

"It wasn't as difficult as one might think. Thank you though. We are both better off for it."

It is dawning on me now that I do not want Carter to ask why we got divorced. The main component; my fertility issues and the demise of our relationship from there.

Luckily, he doesn't press any further.

"It's kind of a slow time of year for me, not a lot to do but wait for harvest and check on shit every day. I was thinking I would come pick you up if you're up for it tomorrow? We could find something to do. Not a lot around here but the lake and Kearney, a town about forty-five minutes north of here, but-"

"I could go to work with you?" I suggest.

He puts his pickup in park outside of his garage and looks over at me.

"You want to come to work with me?" His eyebrows raise, causing small lines to form in his otherwise smooth forehead.

Feeling embarrassed by my unfiltered thought, "I don't have to! I just don't want you to go out of your way for me or anything. I sprung this whole trip on you and you have a life and-"

"Spring anything on me as often as you want, sweetheart."

Carter winks at me as he unbuckles his seatbelt, his tattoo showing off as his muscles work themselves in the small movements. Taken aback by his what-I-want-to-believe-is flirting it takes me a moment to look away from him and unbuckle my own seatbelt. By the time I have myself freed, Carter is opening my door and waiting to walk with me to my car.

"Thank you again for supper and drinks. That really was the best chicken fried steak I've ever had."

"Someday when you have the ones I make, you'll need to lie to me then," he laughs.

I choke a bit at what he just said; implying about a future where that happens.

He doesn't back down though, no backtracking. He holds firm and I can see it in his eyes that he doesn't view what he just said as insane or forward or anything other than hopeful.

"I'll, uh, come back tomorrow? I can bring you lunch?"

His smile grows and my knees shake. He is beautiful.

"Lunch sounds great. Meet me here at noon, I'll find us something to do."

Carter opens my door for me, and I get in. He leans in, one hand on the roof and the other on the door itself.

"I am so glad you showed up here today, Kris Atwater."

"I'm really glad you're glad, Carter Barker."

His eyes soften and dip to my mouth before they pop back to my eyes.

"Watch for deer," he says with a smile as he backs away from my car, shutting my door softly.

Carter watches me turn around in his driveway and pass through the trees, his hands in his front pockets and a smile firmly in place the entire time.

Holy shit, what am I doing? And why does it feel so right?

Chapter Five

What a Man Gotta Do

Carter

*H*oly shit. Wow.

Here I sit, an hour and a half after Kris left my house, on my front porch with a beer and nerves coursing through my body like nobody's business.

She was here. At my house. *In* my house. She rode with me in my pickup. I watched her eat the best chicken fried steak in the state. I drove her back here and she is really... *here*. She's real and she's here and she's single and *holy shit*.

It seems unrealistic to want someone the way I want Kris. I know that if I were to spout off my true, unfiltered feelings to someone they would question my sanity. And I would not even be able to blame them. But in the last five years, through all of the milestones and small moments, she has always been there, in the back of my mind.

Her.

I didn't even know her name until today and any time I would try to put one to her memorable face, they all felt wrong. She was a constant in those late night thoughts or those silent moments of contemplation on a long drive. A quiet, little, bright spot of what-ifs. Any night out with Ken where I let myself get a little too loose, she would become a topic of conversation. It was as though she had become this eighth wonder of the world to me.

And now she's here, no less of a wonder than yesterday, but all the more real.

It's almost ten, but I am so wired I could run a marathon. I pluck my phone off of the table in front of me and dial my best friend.

"Hey good buddy. What's up?"

"She's here."

"I'm going to need more context here, Cars. Who's here?"

"Kris."

My brain cannot comprehend that today actually happened. That I somehow have this chance all of a sudden.

"Who's Kris? Are you having a stroke? Do I need to come over?"

I shake my head to try and get my brain to function properly and hold a conversation. "No, sorry. Okay." I let out a breath. "Kris Atwater. The girl from the concert. The Eric Chur-"

"Yeah, dude. I know who you're talking about now. Are you serious?"

"As a heart attack."

"I'm on my way over."

I knew he would be.

Not twenty minutes later, Ken pulls into my driveway in his dark red Durango.

"Grabbed you a drink," I say as I hold out a bottle of Busch Light to him.

He grabs it and twists the top off. "Alright, go ahead."

I tell Ken about how Kris showed up out of the blue and we went to dinner. About how she is divorced and coming over tomorrow to bring me lunch. He is as shocked as I still am.

"Holy shit, Carter. She just—"

"She just showed up, man."

"And now?"

"And now... I don't know, man. Like, I know it's insane, but I swear to all Ken, she's it for me. I know that's crazy. I knew it was crazy then. I know it still is. But what I don't know is how to stop that feeling from taking over. I need her like I need fucking air, Ken. I want her like I want my next meal. What do I do from here?"

I look across the table at my friend who has seen me through it all. His brown eyes and the wrinkles on the outside corners are one of the only constants I have had in my life. His blonde hair is starting to thin but at thirty-three you would think he was maybe almost thirty. He is slim and built like the quarterback he always was in high school. His nose sits a little crooked on his thin face from the fight he got into our junior year with Matt Hanson. All because Matt was talking shit about how he "stole" my girl from me because he wasn't as poor as me. He wasn't lying, I was broke-broke, but that shit did not need to be broadcasted. So, Ken took care of Matt and got suspended from that weekend's football game. He's the one that has been with me since the beginning. The one who was there when I met Kris all those years ago. He knows how in I was even when I did not have a shot in hell with her.

"What do I do, Ken?"

Ken takes a drink before sitting forward and leaning his elbows on his jean-clad thighs. He spins the bottle in his hands a few times before looking at me and saying, "Whatever you have to do, Cars. That's what you do."

Surprised when I shouldn't be by his absurd support, I laugh and shake my head before finishing my drink and setting the bottle on the floor by my chair.

"Operation Get The Girl?" I laugh.

Ken holds his beer up in a solo salute. "Operation Get The Girl, good buddy."

I am walking next to Ken as he heads towards his car to go home.

"Hey, don't you have Cameron this weekend?"

"Nah, Sadie called today and asked to swap weekends. They're in Omaha for some Disney on Ice thing."

"What did Kris say about you having a two-year-old?"

When I do not answer him, Ken turns around and raises his eyebrows.

"I didn't know how to just, I don't know, come out with that information without it possibly completely freaking her out." I don't look him in the eyes.

I wanted to tell Kris about Cameron. I am proud as fuck about my kid. He is the best thing to ever happen to me. He was not planned but it never mattered to me. He is so damn cool and he is the love of my life. He IS my life. But I feel like I know I have to go about this whole thing with Kris at a weird pace. I need to be careful. She looks ready to run at the first sign of anything borderline off kilter. I don't know what her thoughts on a two-year-old son with a one-night stand would consist of and I am not ready to find out just yet.

"We only spent like, three hours together Ken. Nothing deep came up other than her stating that she was no longer married."

Ken puts his hand on my shoulder and says to me, "Buddy, tell the girl about your kid. Don't fuck around with that kind of information."

He's right.

"You're right. I will. First thing tomorrow."

"Good man. Talk at you later."

"Drive safe, man."

Chapter Six

Be My Baby Tonight

Carter

I woke up this morning feeling like I got a full ten hours of sleep. When, in reality, I got six. My brain would not shut off. It would not leave me alone. All of the potential scenarios circled like water in a never ending drain. All. Night. Long.

Kris is here, in Nebraska, but for how long? Is she here for a friendship or more than that? Have I made it clear enough that even though I know nothing about her, I know she is it for me? What if she hates kids? What if she wants more kids, and what if when I tell her I am one-and-done, that's a deal breaker? What if it turns out she is a mass murderer and kills me in my sleep after a night of rocking each other's worlds?

What a way to go.

My body is tired, and my brain needs rest, but the unanswered questions are too loud for any reprieve. So here I am, changing the oil in my pickup while I wait for noon to arrive and with it, Kris Atwater.

I hear tires on the gravel while I finish pouring new oil into its home under the hood of my truck. I look down at my left wrist, checking the time on my black Apple Watch.

"Eleven-thirty, missed me that much, Kris?" I say playfully without looking at her, a smile pulling at my lips.

"I texted you two hours ago, Carter."

I freeze. That... is not Kris.

I poke my head around my truck and my stomach bottoms out, my heart rate picks up.

"Dad!!"

Shit.

The last bit of oil spills over the engine as I jerk to stand up fully. "Shit, shit, shit!"

"Dad! Bad word!" Cameron hollers from his tricycle on the sidewalk by the porch.

"Cars, you all good?" Sadie asks while coming to the front of my pickup.

"All good Sadie," I say as I wipe my hands off with the blue shop towels I have sitting next to my feet. "I haven't checked my phone since I started all of this," I motion to the oil everywhere. "So, I didn't know you were bringing Cam over. Everything good with Lance?"

She waves me off and turns to go to Cameron. "Everything's good. The show last night was great. Lance got called into the plant. Something about an emergency shut down. So, Cameron and I came back this morning. I'll probably head back to Omaha this afternoon."

I walk over to my kid, smiling and no longer stressed about the what if's. I reach down and pluck him off his bike and he squeals and giggles as I tickle his little toddler tummy.

"Bubba, I missed you." I say as I rub my scruff over his stomach. That always makes him laugh extra hard. "Did you miss me kid?"

He is laughing too hard to answer. As I set him back on the ground, I plant a big kiss on his little lips, squishing his cheeks in between my large hands. He bats me away while laughing still and hops back on his bike.

"All good then, Cars?"

"All good, Sades. Thanks for bringing him home."

She winks, "You bet, bud. Got plans this weekend?"

Shit. I should probably tell Sadie about Kris. Right? She told me about her Lance when they started talking. I should definitely bring up my Kris.

My Kris.

"Hey, Sades. I have to talk to you about something."

She pauses mid step on the way back to her white Traverse. Turning around to face me, her eyebrows nearly in her hairline.

"It's uh," I rub the back of my sweaty neck with my dirty hand.

I need a shower.

"Cars?" Concern drips from the nickname.

"Yeah, sorry. Okay. So, here's the thing." How do I tell the mother of my child that I am probably in love with someone I do not even know, and that that someone is going to be pulling into my driveway any minute now and I don't have a way to call her to tell her to not come or to wait until nap time in two hours or to just give her a heads up because as I mentioned before, I do not fucking know the woman, let alone her phone number.

Fuck.

"Okay. Here goes nothing. Five years ago, I met this woman in South Dakota at a concert with Ken. She was married and I left it at that, nothing happened but I gave her my name. She showed up yesterday and is no longer married and I know it's insane, trust me I *know*, but I think I could probably love this woman for the rest of my life and she's going to be here any minute because I made plans with her today when I thought that Cammy wouldn't be here until tomorrow evening and I don't know what to do here."

I loose a breath and reign in my nerves. Or try to. Sadie is looking at me like I am clinically insane, and maybe I am. I am fully aware of how all of this sounds. Of how it has sounded for years. Every time Ken or I brought up the mystery-woman-now-Kris, the feelings were still the same.

I can see the questions in Sadie's brown eyes. She's beautiful. She always was and as the mother of my child, always will be. She is a classic kind of pretty. Her naturally brown hair lays in waves past her shoulders. Her face is nearly always bare, and her freckles were the first thing I noticed when we met at a bar in Kearney. She is five-foot six; I know from doctors' appointments when she was pregnant.

She is kind and relaxed. I could not be luckier in the baby-mama department. We went on one date, had sex, mutually decided we were better suited to being just friends or at least friendly. Three months later she called me to tell me she was pregnant. She wanted nothing from me other than for me to have that knowledge, but I would never have left the responsibility of a child to be solely hers. Or anyone's. So, we started doing a weekly coffee get together. Not a date. We never once tried or let or make things go in a romantic direction. But we got together once a week to get to know one another. To figure out how we were going to fit into each other's lives for the rest of our lives. We decided early on that we would do this together without being together. I was at every appointment. Financially I did what we agreed on. We got everything finalized through a judge to cover our bases and it has been the smoothest sailing since.

Now, with Cameron being two and a half, we co-parent better than anyone I know. She is one of my best friends, honestly.

"Wait," Sadie finally says, waving her manicured hand in the air. "Is this THE mystery woman I've heard you mention?"

"One and the same," I say on a breath. "And she'll be here," I look down at my watch. "In like, now." I look back up to Sadie. She is smiling widely with her arms crossed over her chest.

"Well, I'll be. This is going to be so much fun."

What.

"What?" I ask, confused by her amusement.

"You have never brought a girl home, Cars. In the three years I've known you, you haven't even dated. You've done your thing," she winks at me, "Of course, but nothing was ever serious, and no one has ever stood a chance at meeting Cameron and infiltrating your structured life."

Feeling like I no longer have time to beat around the bush I tell Sadie, "She doesn't know about Cameron. Not because I don't want her to, that would be fucking insane. But I just didn't want to freak her out last night and I was nerv-"

"I get it. You're fine, Cars. Relax. I'll take Cameron for the weekend; Lance can come to Kearney if he wants. You take the weekend to figure out your new love-life." Sadie laughs at me as she walks to where Cameron is sitting with the chalk on the driveway. "Cam, we're going to go home but you'll come back to dads in a few days, okay?" She swoops him up into a hug.

Cameron's bottom lip juts out and my heart breaks. I don't know what I am doing here. Sadie is not wrong. I have *never* brought a girl home to Cameron before. But I need to do this right. For him. For Kris.

I ruffle his brown hair and kiss him on the cheek as they walk by me. "I love you bud. I'll call you tonight, okay?"

"Luh you," he says as his mom tickles his squishy tummy.

"I want to know EVERYTHING, Carter Arlington Francis Barker," Sadie hollers over her shoulder as she gets in her car. "Everything." Her smile does not fade, and I can tell she is laughing at my stress as she pulls out of the driveway.

And not a moment too soon because by the time I am back to my garage, picking up and putting away all of my oil changing shit, I hear tires on the gravel again. It is like my body has this awareness to her. This draw. I know it's her before I even turn around to see. When it was Sadie, I was unsure. Not now.

"Hey stranger," I say with my back to her as she closes her door, washing my hands in the sink in my garage. "Do not fuck this up," I whisper to myself.

Chapter Seven

This Kiss

Kris

No one on God's green Earth has the right to look so damn fine in nothing but a crusty pair of blue jeans and a black wrinkled, holey t-shirt. It definitely has nothing to do with the grease he is washing off his strong hands with that gritty orange shop soap. No, it is certainly not the way his dark hair is sticking up in a few places like he has been running his dirty hands through it all morning. Surely it is not attractive how he has got smudges of grime on his scruffy cheeks or the way his sunglasses hang on the back of the stretched-out neck of his t-shirt. I have certainly not noticed his biceps flexing, those wings moving, as he dries his hands off now with a blue paper towel and then runs it over his glistening face.

Holy shit... I am so screwed.

I hear him chuckle and my heart ceases its beating for a moment. It's as if it is halting all operations so that we can soak in the sound of the laugh coming from the beautiful man's chest two yards away.

I clear my throat, shake my head slightly, and tell myself to sack up. He is just a man. I am just a woman. Chill.

I am anything but chill.

"I didn't know what you like to eat so I got you a hamburger and onion rings. But then I got myself a chicken sandwich with fries. So, we can totally swap or switch or split or whatever you want because I'll eat any of it. I had them put the mayo and stuff on the side because I don't like mayo, but I didn't know if you did so I figured better safe than sorry, and also there's a slice of cheese in here too because I don't like cheese on my sandwiches, really only on pizza. Like, how it gets kind of crispy and not gooey and weird. So, I didn't have them put it on either of the sandwiches but in case you're a cheese kind of dude, there's a slice in here and also pickles and a couple sides of ranch and I got you an iced tea but also a coke and you can have either, or both. You could have both." I slow down and inhale deeply before looking up from the brown paper bag I am holding.

Carter is leaning against the frame of his open garage, his arms crossed against his broad chest and one ankle over the other with one booted foot balancing on its toes. His blue eyes are filled with amusement and his smile makes me feel wholly inappropriate things.

I smile slightly and take a breath. "Hi."

"Hi," he replies, his voice smooth and light.

"Hi," I say again. "That was a lot. I brought us lunch." I hold up the large brown paper bag.

He laughs again and I die a little inside. How can someone's laugh be so attractive?

"I see that," he says as he strides towards me, an amused grin on his tan face.

He stops once he is close enough that his chest is nearly touching the sack of food. Reaching out his hands, he takes the bag and nods his head towards his house.

"We can eat inside. Go on in, I'll follow."

"Oh, no. I hate walking in front of someone or going in somewhere first."

He doesn't hesitate or laugh or outwardly judge me. Most would. Most do. I have these things. These insecurities that cause me to ramble or freeze. Things that make me not want to walk into a room first or lead a line or walk in front of someone. He does not even bat an eye at my weird "things'.

"Well, come on Kris Atwater. Let's see what we've got going on in here," Carter says from the steps on his porch with a smile.

Lead the way, stud.

After splitting both sandwiches and fries and onion rings, full bellies and laughing happily at the small details I am learning about Carter, I feel so... content.

He played football in Wilcox grade two through twelve. He wanted to wrestle but his mom told him no. He likes ranch on anything and everything. His parents are both deceased, they had him super late in life as a "happy accident", and passed away within a year of each other. He is at peace with the whole thing which is both wild and admirable. He has all of two friends that he speaks to on a regular basis, Ken who I know of and then someone named Sadie. He got a bit cagey at his accidental mention of her, but the conversation kept going on. He is in fact six-foot two, thirty-two-years-old, and he looks like his dad did when he was young.

"I need to go check on my cows. Is that something you're in to?" he asks while pulling his boots back on at the kitchen table.

I let out an embarrassing squeal of excitement before reigning it in and feigning indifference. "Yeah, sure. I could tag along if you want." I shrug my shoulders, fooling no one at all.

Carter laughs and heads towards his front door. "Let's get going then, sweetheart."

My heart skips a beat at the name he has used twice now.

Once in his pickup, a steady flow of ninety's country music as the background noise, Carter pulls out onto the main gravel road and goes north, away from the highway.

"How many cows do you have? Are they Angus? Do you breed them yourself or do AI? Do you sell them after they grow, or do you keep them for the beef?"

I rattle off the questions, unable to squash my excitement. I love livestock. Cows. Horses. Pigs. Sheep.

Anything but chickens.

Carter laughs at my assault of an interrogation before answering. "I have about forty-five head year-round. Sixty percent are black Angus, the rest are Charol-"

"You have Charolais?! Those are my absolute favorite!" I pin my hands under my thighs and force myself to try and sit still. I like to think I have played it semi-cool so far, but that façade is quickly falling, and Carter here is about to see just how spazzy ol' Kris Katherine Atwater can be over "moo cows" as I have always (and refuse to give up) called them.

I turn my head to look at him after a moment of quiet and what I find stalls my breathing.

He has slowed the pickup down to a crawl, nearing a small driveway and gate. His eyes are steady and happy, sparkling with amusement. But not the judgmental make-fun-of-someone kind of amused. It's like there is a genuine interest in what he is look at. His smile is wide and the wrinkles at the corners of his eyes are extra deep in this moment.

"You are so fucking cute."

Swoon.

"I'm embarrassing and aggressively excited at best, but thank you," I say while laughing.

Carter shakes his head, his smile not wavering.

"You're cute and I love that you are excited about something as simple as cows. Now, where was... Yes, okay. Angus and Charolais. I let the cows do their own thing with the two bulls I have and just hope for the best. I do sell most, and usually keep one back for myself and Ken."

"And you farm?"

He nods his head, "You bet. We don't know much about one another huh? I don't know at all what you do." He turns his pickup into the little grassy driveway that goes into a field. "Hold that thought," he says as he hops out to open the gate.

I shamelessly watch the entire process. I watch his dump truck of a butt in his work jeans as he walks to the barbed wire gate. I watch his arms and back flex as he pulls the hoop-lock system off a post. I watch the way he walks the gate across the entrance and then sets it on the ground, wiping his hands on the front of his pants and inspecting the ground for anything that might cause issues to his pickup.

It is like farm-boy porn.

I understand it is August in Nebraska and it is damn near one hundred degrees but suddenly the AC in this truck is not helping the heat rushing through my body.

None of that, not even his eye contact as he walks back to his seat and gets in, stops me from continuing my perusal.

As I said, shameless.

"Twenty questions."

I am pulled back to reality and out of fantasizing about how his scruff would feel against my neck.

"Huh?" My green eyes look into his blue ones. They are almost a navy blue color. Deep but bright.

Focus.

"Let's play twenty questions," Carter says again, his knowing smile making mine grow. "I'll start, we take turns, learn about each other."

"Yeah, that sounds good. Go ahead. Make it count." I wink at him.

Who is this brazen Kris and when did she get here?

He laughs as he pulls into the lot and drives down a hill. I can see a tall windmill and a silver water tank, no cows.

Carter clears his throat before asking, "What do you do for work?"

"I do web designing. I work for a small but super great company that stays busy enough to be successful. We do designs for grocery stores and other kinds of stores. It's remote so I can do it from any-where, which was the immediate appeal. After doing it for the last seven years though, I can't imagine doing anything else or working for anyone else."

He smiles at me before turning his attention back to the road. "Looks like the girls are all on the other side of the lot. We can circle back tonight to see if they're back. Your turn."

Shoot... a question... any question...

"Do you have a girlfriend?"

I feel the truck jerk to a stop and when I put my attention on Carter, he looks surprised.

We haven't discussed his love life. Just mine in the way that I blurted out my divorced status.

"You're serious?" His tone is not irritated, but just confused and shocked.

"Yes?" I hedge, shrugging my shoulders.

He puts the pickup in park right here on the top of the hill we were cresting to go back out the way we came. He unbuckles and turns his body fully to me, leaning back against his door with one leg pulled up on to his seat slightly. I do the same, not having the slightest idea of what is happening but rolling with it.

"Alright, I had assumed that it was clear where I stood here but let me make it super clear now."

His tone is not condescending. It is not a reprimanding kind of thing. He is being sincere and transparent and kind and that does a lot to my heart.

"I am single. The single-est. I have been for years. Even before I met you all those years ago, I didn't do a lot of relationships. For no reason other than being busy and not finding someone that I wanted that sort of commitment with. And then I saw you. I met you and you can ask Ken when you see him, because you will, that was it for me, Kris. My heart hasn't beat so hard since that night in Sioux Falls. That was, until you showed up on my porch yesterday afternoon." He winks, I blush. "So, full disclosure and at serious risk of freaking you out but taking my shot anyways, this is where I am at Kris. I like you. I know I don't know you and you don't know me, and I understand that it is wild to spout the whole 'love at first sight' thing, but I waited twenty-seven years to meet you and I've waited five more years for you to find me again. I would have waited my whole life for you to show up on my front porch. I'm happy as hell that I didn't have to wait that long. And again, I know it's insane, but I am drawn to you. It's like my heart beats for yours. My soul is tied to yours. My being was created for *yours*. I'm looking at you here; in *my* pickup, in *my* field, in *my* town, and I am floored that you're real. And I won't lie or hide these feelings because that would be a genuine disservice to you and to me, Kris. So, yeah, I'm single. And in the same breath my heart has belonged to you for the last five years somehow. You could take it clean out of my chest and I would say thank you."

He exhales deeply, as if that entire speech had been trying to break free for years. And maybe it had because wow...

"I-" I cut myself off. What do you say to that? He all but told me he loves me, and we have not spent a total of twenty-four hours together yet.

But... The main reason I don't know what to say is because none of what he said sounded crazy to me. I mean, crazy in a what-are-these-feelings kind of way, yes. But not crazy in a you-need-institutionalized kind of way.

Crazy in a... this all makes sense and feels right, kind of way.

"So," he says, "I don't know what you want out of life or this," he gestures between us. "But I have never wanted to get to know someone for the rest of my life as badly as I want to get to know you."

"Yes," I breathe out, little more than a whisper.

His blue eyes widen, the dark lashes nearly touching his brows, and I let myself smile fully.

Do something for YOU, Kris.

"Yes?" he asks.

"Yes. I want to know you. Desperately, if I'm being honest. I don't think I'm as good with words as you are, that was incredible to hear. I wish I would have written it down. But yes, Carter Barker, thirty-three now, Ragan, Nebraska. If you think it's, whatever this," I wave my hand between us, "is one sided, it isn't. My marriage was over long, long before it ended, and I would be lying if I said I hadn't thought of you, probably too often, over the last five years. And it is crazy and fast and a bit wild but honestly, I've done the safe and the sane and the proper shit my whole life Carter. I think I could go for some crazy."

"Kris, I'm going to be real honest-"

"Is that supposed to sound like something new?" I laugh.

He moves closer, smiling broadly, putting his head and upper body above his center console. I do the same, bringing my face just inches away from his. The smell of chewing tobacco and minty gum caress my senses. Carter brings his right hand up to the side of my face and I lean into his touch in a what-should-be alarmingly natural way. His thumb brushes my flushed cheek and I close my eyes. I feel his breath on my mouth as his other hand comes up to grip the other side of my face. His fingertips tangle in the back of my pulled-up hair, causing goosebumps to erupt over my entire body.

"I'm going to kiss you now, yeah?" His voice is but a whisper on my skin.

"I wish you would."

And he does. God bless, he does. Carter I-need-to-learn-his-middle-name Barker kisses like a fucking spring storm, washing away everything from the before. It's soft and slow at first, light. And then...

And then.

It all picks up. My heart rate, the heat, my feelings. An emotion I cannot quite explain envelopes me.

It is foot popping and life altering, this kiss. It is lightning and thunder, peace and quiet. It is your favorite song playing on vinyl during the early hours of a fall day while you drink the perfect cup of coffee and read your favorite book. That is what this is.

Not even just this kiss; *it is Carter.*

He is this feeling of complete and utter... belonging.

Chapter Eight

Things Dads Do

Carter

Fireworks. Cliché and expected but holy shit...

Kris fucking Atwater is *it*.

My heart is nearly beating out of my chest. I can feel her smile against my kiss-swollen lips as we pause what has to be the best first kiss to have ever happened to anyone.

"That," she breathes into my mouth. She must have forgotten her train of thought, she goes quiet.

I will not even pretend that her lack of words does not do something to my ego.

"Yeah," I whisper back.

I run a hand down the front of her neck, moving across her collarbone and trailing lightly down her arm. She's got her hands in my hair at the back of my head. As I make my way down the length of her smooth forearm, I grasp her hand and pull it from behind my head to my mouth. I press soft kisses to each finger, pausing to look down at the delicate silver band engraved with little daisies on her fourth finger. I send a silent "thank you" to God that this is her right hand.

"My brother and his fiancé got that for me after my divorce was finalized."

"It's pretty." I kiss her ringed finger.

Her forehead rests against mine and we sit there for a few moments, silently soaking in each other's nearness. I hold her hand to my chest, letting her feel how hard my heart is beating for her. Opening my eyes, I am rewarded with her half lidded green ones looking back at me.

"You're beautiful," I whisper.

Her cheeks turning a soft pink makes me want to say it a hundred times more, but I refrain.

"Twenty questions." I remind both of us. I have a question I have wanted to ask since yesterday when she stood outside of my house, finally within reach. But I definitely do not want to scare her off. I remember then, *transparency*. So, I buck up. "Are you planning on staying?"

I'm terrified of her answer. I want to say I would sell my cows, my house, my fucking pickup and move my whole life to wherever she is. I *want* to say that. But then I think of Cameron not even a millisecond later, and I think of his beautiful little face and then I remember that Kris does not even know about him yet and my pulse picks up and the panic starts to set in and-

"Come back," Kris whispers, rubbing her thumb where her hand is pressed to my chest. "Come back."

I nod, taking a steadying breath. Less than a day of knowing each other and she can already ground me. She can sense the anxiety, or the churning, and she has the power over me to bring me back to her.

"Where'd you go?"

"Nowhere," I fib. "I just..."

"I'm staying. For the next few weeks at least."

Weeks? That isn't enough. Fuck, years would not cut it. My eyes widen and my body flinches. I sit back, immediately missing the touch of her.

"Hold on," Kris says calmly.

"Sorry. Go on." I'm trying to not freak out, but I need time here, man. I need time to sort it out and tell her about Cameron and feel out that situation because I will not leave my kid and I cannot just throw Kris into stepmom life like that.

A declaration of basically-love is one thing. A whole kid is another thing entirely.

"I have to go back to North Dakota for my things at some point, in like, the distant future. If that's..." Kris pauses, chewing on her bottom lip. I want to pull it out from between her teeth and kiss her worries away. "If that's what we decide-"

"Yes." I do not hesitate once I know where she is going with that. "I want you. Here. I want you and I want you here. I'll pay your rent or whatever, or you can move into one of the spare rooms in my house. Whatever you want Kris. I'll do whatever you want, sweetheart."

Fuck being afraid of scaring her off apparently.

Kris laughs and I beg anyone and everyone that might be listening to allow me the chance of hearing that melodic sound until the day I die.

"I can cover my own rent, Carter," she says while still laughing. She sits back in her seat, righting herself.

I follow suit, settling into the driver's seat and fixing my shirt that slid up my torso. I glance over to see Kris eying the bit of skin that was showing and it takes a considerable amount of effort to not just take the whole shirt off, give her a real show.

I am not as fit as I once was. Definitely not as hairless either. Somewhere between cowboy and dad-bod. But if Kris likes what she sees, I will not change a damn thing.

We both face forward again, small smiles tipping our lips up. I put my pickup in to drive and take us out of the field. Once the gate is back up and locked, and I'm sitting behind the wheel, I pause to look at Kris. She is studying one of her light pink nails, inspecting a chip maybe. I watch her. Lord, I could do just that for an eternity.

But instead of hiding my truth and acting like a coward, I clear my throat and her eyes find mine. I give her a small smile. "I need to tell you something. And please, *please* don't freak out because it is a big deal but he's like, so cool, Kris. Seriously. Cameron is the end all and be all of awesome. He's beautiful and good and funny and he can damn near run a combine all by himself. Well, not really because that would be dangerous, but he will be able to in like, seven years. And-"

Kris holds her hand up, silencing my ramble, and then places it on my bicep. I look at my hands, my knuckles white while gripping the steering wheel.

"Slow down, cowboy."

I can hear the amusement but the slight undertone of concern in her voice.

Fuck.

What if she doesn't like kids? What if she does not want them, even if it is one she doesn't have to carry or whatever? What if-

"Who is Cameron?"

I look over at her, releasing my grip and smiling at the thought of my sweet kid.

"He's my son."

Chapter Nine

Mama, I'm Alright

Kris

"He's my son."

"What?" I sputter.

Listen. I do *not* care that Carter has a son. I don't care that he is just now telling me. I don't honestly know what exactly it is I care about in this moment.

Yes, I do.

I am not a mom. I am not *meant* to be a mom. My uterus made sure of that. She decided that I would not get that chance. And while it crushed me to know all of that, to learn it in painful and mentally taxing ways, I have adjusted. I have accepted and grieved and moved on with the fact that I will never be any sort of a "mom".

"I'm sorry I didn't tell you the minute you walked through my front door. Yesterday or today. I didn't know how to just casually drop that into your lap and I also didn't want to scare you off before I could see what we were doing here and-"

"Stop." It comes out a little more abrupt than I had intended but my brain is computing and calculating and thinking far too quickly for anything else right now.

I hold my hand up.

Quiet. I need...

Carter sinks into his chair. His face is solemn but sure and I do not doubt for a second that he is a great father. Carter is a good man.

"I need a second."

"Sure, yeah. Take whatever time you need. I'll get us home." His voice is soft and sure. His grip on the steering wheel, however, looks strained.

The drive to his house is quiet and full of tension. I have a million and one feelings coursing through me.

He is a dad. He has routines and a life, he is responsible for another *person's* life. And who is the mom? What were her and Carter in the beginning? What are they now? He has a whole son, and I could never get past thirteen weeks of being pregnant.

I settled with the fact that kids were not in my future. The thought of adoption was fine but just not something I was going to do alone as my marriage failed, and who wants to be with someone who is essentially "broken" and unable to have children? And then a stepchild never occurred to me because, well, see previous comment. I had settled with it all. That I was going to be "alone" for forever and that I would be the best aunt this universe had ever seen. I have so much love to give and always wanted children to give it to, but I was fine— AM fine, with it being given to nieces and nephews someday when Bryce has little babies running around.

I am fine.

Carter parks his truck, and I am brought back to this reality, the thousands of thoughts running through my brain going down in volume ever so slightly. I cannot imagine what he thinks about me going fucking catatonic in here upon hearing about his son.

Cameron.

"Cameron."

I didn't mean to say it aloud but Carter's gaze whips to mine as I turn to look at him.

"Yeah," he smiles. "Cameron Carter Barker."

"What's your middle name?"

The question takes us both by surprise. Lightening the mood slightly, Carter smirks.

"I've got two."

"Overachiever?" I huff a laugh.

This is going fine. It's all fine.

Carter laughs back. "My parents wanted it to mean something, my name. So, Carter is just because they liked it and at the time no one in this small Midwest area would share the same name. Arlington was my dad's dads first name. Francis was my mom's dad's middle name."

"Carter Arlington Francis Barker." I say it softly. It feels good on my tongue, around my teeth. I think I notice a small shiver run through Carter's arms but I don't mention it.

"Come on, let's talk on the porch. I'll grab a couple drinks."

We both climb out of his pickup, walking up the small, paved way to his beautiful porch. I see the tricycle and kick myself for not even asking if he had kids, especially when I asked if he was single.

As Carter comes out with a couple bottles of beer, taking a seat next to me on his little outdoor couch, I ask him, "Wait, you said you hardly dated, like ever?"

Carter takes a long drink and nods his head. "Yeah, Cameron's mom and I didn't date. Her name is Sadie-"

"The Sadie you mentioned as one of your best friends?!" I try to not choke on my beer.

Carter just laughs before looking at me. "Yes, the one and same. She's great. But we, the two of us, in a romantic way... That was never a thing."

"I'm going to need some more context here, babe."

His eyes go serious as they bore into mine. "Say it again." His voice is barely audible.

"What?" I lean away slightly, narrowing my eyes in question. "Babe?"

He nods and his body relaxes. His free hand moves to my knee, and he squeezes where it lands.

"Yeah," he whispers. "That."

I won't dive into that at this moment. I let it rock, let it roll. Moving on, I ask again, "Okay, so Sadie? She's Cameron's mom?"

He shakes his head like he is shaking himself back to Earth. "Yeah, yes. Sadie. She's Cameron's mom. He'll be three in February. Her and I hooked up one night and that kid just wanted to be born because regardless of the, uh," he rubs the back of his neck, the heat from his palm on my knee is immediately missed. "The measures taken that night didn't prevent him from being conceived, I guess. So, Sadie contacted me a few months after and let me know what was going on. We were both super good about communicating the lack of feelings either of us had for the other. We've just been coparenting and learning as we go for the last couple of years. He's getting older now and so he's here more than he was when he was a baby but Cameron's..."

Carter breathes deeply and smiles softly.

"He's awesome. He's cute and funny and smart and brave and he's the love of my life."

I feel a pang of jealousy at that. Not at Carter claiming Cameron to be the love of his life, he *should* feel that way. It is insanely hot that he feels that way. But the fact that I will never have a small, little human being to fall in love with like that... that makes my vision almost green.

I swallow down my hurt. "He sounds incredible." And I mean it. Cameron does sound wonderful.

Carter bumps his shoulder into mine, both of us leaning more into each other.

I need to tell him. I need him to know where I stand on the whole childbearing thing, or lack thereof. If he at some point wants more children, even though that is wayyyyy down the line for us, if there is an us... Like when we have known each other for two weeks or something, he needs to know now what that all looks like for me.

"I nee-"

"Do you-"

We laugh at ourselves as we speak at the same time.

"You go first," Carter says.

I swallow once, twice. I take a steadying breath.

This is what changed it all for Michael.

Broken. Broken. Broken.

That thought echoes in my head, the words he said to me as our marriage crumbled. Until the tears start to line my eyes.

Carter notices. That is what he does, I think. He *sees*.

"Sweetheart," he whispers as he sets his beer down, taking mine from my clenched fists. He moves the table that sits in front of us and gets down on his knees, leaning forward onto mine. Taking both of my hands in his and kissing the tops of each he says, "Kris, you can tell me anything."

And I believe him. This man. Gosh... This man. He is just that; a man. He is kind and good and smart and professional and handsome and *trustworthy*. And I truly believe I know all of that just from the last two days of seeing him again. Not a single part of me thinks that the craziness of it all can take away from any of it.

"I can't have children," I whisper, not making eye contact.

"I'm going to need more here, sweetheart. To understand it all— if you can do that, that is. I'd love more but don't feel like you need to give it all away now. Okay?"

I inhale and exhale a few times, deeply and unsteadily. This is it. This is something that changed the foundation of my marriage. It changed the way the man I married, a man I thought loved me endlessly, looked at me. He thought I was damaged, somehow. Like I wasn't complete anymore. Like without a fully functioning womb—

I shake away Michael's words and the pitying but disgusted look in his eyes.

"I can't have children. Biologically. I can't carry a baby to term." My words are sure, but my voice is somber.

"How-," Carter cuts himself off and takes a breath. "I mean, you're sure? Obviously, you're sure, but like-"

His question is not nosy to me. It does not feel that way, at least. It's a small push. A gentle shove to go on. To give it all to him.

"I have been pregnant five times." Carter tries to keep it to himself, but I hear his sharp inhale. I don't stop though. "Each time I made it to anywhere from ten to thirteen weeks. Each time I miscarried and each time a part of me died with the process. After the fifth I finally told my ex-husband I had to be done. I couldn't do it anymore. I couldn't keep trying. I couldn't keep going through all of the testing and the timing of sex and the words of sympathy from nurses over the phone telling me what I already knew. I couldn't take another month of *scheduling* intimacy all to finish the job and then lay there by myself with my feet hanging in the air against the wall in an effort to like, keep things in." I cringe. "I could barely go to the restroom anytime I was pregnant without bursting into tears. I would go pee and inspect the toilet paper each time just praying to

God, and anyone else that might be listening to my pleas, for there to not be even the smallest speck of blood. And every time, by the end of each one, there it would be. And it was horrible. It was so horrible."

I choke on a sob. Even though I *am* fine with the way things have gone, with the lack of child bearing I can achieve... Discussing the losses I went through is so difficult. Carter sits back down next to me and brings me onto his lap, wrapping his large arms around me. I peek out from my hands that cover my face.

"I'm going to squish you, Carter. I'm not sit-on-his-lap small." My words are muffled from the snot trying to run into my mouth.

I should be embarrassed. I should be mortified that my size-twenty-ass can simply not be comfortable for him to hold within his large but not *large* frame. The tears streaming down my face and the accompanying boogers are the furthest thing from attractive. Not to mention the literal sob story I just told him... But yet, I feel nothing but... *calm*. Nerves for the man holding me tightly to him, but nothing in the realm of bad.

He brings his hands to my face as I sit up and pull away slightly. His calloused thumbs wipe away my tears and I disgustingly use my t-shirt to remove the rest of the hazardous materials from under my nose.

"You," Carter says, his eyes baring down deep into mine, "Fit just fine, sweetheart."

He leans his face in, his mouth connecting to the middle of my brow. Then each tear-soaked cheek, my surely red nose, before settling on my lips. I gasp slightly and feel his smile form on my mouth.

These are the kind of kisses that heal. The kind of kiss that your mom gave your knee after you scraped it going too fast on your bike around the corner of your street. They are the kind of kisses that warm your heart. That melt your body down to the very base of itself, the simplest and purest form of you. These kisses weld things back together after having been shattered for so long. Mending and fixing, that's what these kisses are doing.

After a few more of those special kisses and a long stretch of quiet, Carter pulls back. He runs his hands up and down my arms, kneading them as he goes. My eyes fall shut and he shakes with a silent laugh.

"I'm so sorry."

My eyes open slowly at his apology.

"It's honestly okay, Carter. It is. It's sad, but it's okay." I say while searching his eyes. I hope to convey the acceptance I hold now. "Not everyone is meant to be a mom, not in the once-was traditional sense. Or carry their own child. There are so many other ways now to be a mother for women that choose to or can't carry a baby. Adoption, fostering, being an aunt that is more involved than they probably should be, but the actual parents don't mind or have the heart to tell her to back off so it's all fine." I laugh slightly, trying to lighten the heavy mood. "So really, I am okay. I accepted it all. I grieved the motherhood I will never have and the babies I loved and still love. I grieved the life I thought I would have and got mad and sad and then came to terms with it all." I breathe deeply. I put my eyes on Carter's, looking directly into him and say, "I am okay with it."

He breathes out and nods his head.

"You, Kris- wait. What's your middle name?" His eyebrows pinch together.

I laugh. "Katherine."

His smile grows and he says, "You, Kris Katherine Atwater are the strongest woman I have ever met. And I am so glad you are here with me now."

My smile widens as we lean in to continue those sweet, soft, healing kisses.

I really am okay with it all, I remind myself. Questioning still what kind of role I could ever have with Carter's son. But I will live in the now and that can all be something tomorrow Kris will tackle.

Chapter Ten

It's All Because of You

Carter

Kris and I sit like this for a while longer, her butt in my lap settled between my legs. Her now-bare feet rest crossed at the ankle on the other end of my outdoor couch. I've got my black sock-clad feet propped up on the table in front of us and my hands run up and down Kris's arm that is not touching my chest. Her arms are curled up in front of her and she has her head resting on my shoulder, her forehead pressed to my neck.

"You smell nice," Kris whispers after a long stretch of comfortable silence.

I pick my head up off of where it was laying on hers and look down. "Oh, yeah?" I smirk.

She rolls her eyes and nods.

"I don't want to meet Cameron yet. If-" she cuts herself off before continuing. "If that's something you've been thinking about."

"It's one of the only things I've been thinking about, sweetheart. But I agree, I think it's best that we wait that step out a bit. Not that I don't want-"

"No, no. I totally agree. People shouldn't be meeting other people's kids all willy-nilly."

I chuckle at her word choice. She pops up to sit back a bit, looking me in the eyes.

Gosh, I could look into her eyes for an insane amount of time and never find everything there is to see in her. I have it bad. But I won't tell her that just yet. I all-but did earlier, but the phrase itself might scare her off and if there is one thing I will not be doing, it is running this incredible woman off just because I jumped the gun.

"We'll wait until it feels right. I'll get him from daycare Tuesday afternoon and then he's with me until Thursday. And then it'll probably be my weekend again Friday after work until Monday morning." My chest hurts from the stress of knowing I will not see Kris in all of that time. "That's a long-"

"It's fine. It's only a few days in the grand scheme of things." Kris's smile settles my pulse.

"Yeah, it is fine." I lean in and kiss her.

"And we still have tonight and tomorrow," she says against my lips.

"That we do." I smile widely, pressing our foreheads together. "No one delivers around here so what do you say about a trip to Kearney for supper?"

"That sounds good."

"*That's* what Raising Cane's is?" Kris all but hollers at me from her seat in my pickup.

Her seat. It is still so surreal that she is here. That the girl I am fairly sure I have loved for five years, is sitting here. In my pickup, in my state, smiling at *me*.

I cannot help but laugh at her. Her eyes were so wide the second she took her first bite of the chicken. She hadn't even tasted the Cane's sauce yet, but when she did, I was sure I was about to watch her have some sort of religious experience.

"That's Cane's, alright. Pretty good, huh?" I smile while we drive south to go home.

"It was better than good. Holy shit, Carter. That sauce!" She throws her head back and sighs. "I could eat that every day for the rest of my life, Carter. And I am not kidding."

Her face is anything but joking and I truly think she believes that.

"Wait until I introduce you to a Runza," I say. "Then you'll never want to leave."

Her face gets even more serious, and I try to not panic at the elephant I just let into the cab of this vehicle.

"Well," she says, "I don't anticipate wanting to leave anyways right now so save your Runza for a rainy day."

We both laugh small chuckles. "It's All Because of You" by Tyler Barham comes through the radio on my shuffled playlist and Kris all but jumps out of her seat.

"I love this song!" she yells before singing along.

God. Bless. She can sing.

What did I do in this life to have deserved this? To have been put in a world in which I get to meet, and now get to know this incredible woman. The way her eyes close as she sings unabashedly. The way she uses the chapstick from my cup holder as a makeshift microphone. The way her voice, deep but angelic, never misses a note or beat or word.

As the song ends and she sets the yellow capped Burt's Bees back down, she looks over at me. I would have pulled over to watch her if I knew it would not have made it weird. Her bare, freckled cheeks turn the most beautiful shade of pink and it takes everything in me to not lean over and pull her face to mine.

"Please don't ever stop singing like that."

She laughs. "Like what?"

"Like you couldn't give a single fuck who saw you or heard you or what anyone thinks of you. Don't ever stop doing that. Don't ever stop not caring because that, sweetheart, was the most incredible concert I've ever been to."

She twists a piece of hair around her finger and smiles down at her feet.

"Thank you," Kris says quietly.

"You can D.J. if it means you'll sing like that again." I hand her my phone. "Please."

Kris does not hesitate before taking my phone and turning on Miranda Lambert. And I swear to all, if I died right now; the last thing I see being this woman and the last thing I hear being the voice that maybe would maybe not win American Idol, but definitely would win my vote; I would not even be remotely mad.

My headstone could read *"Carter Barker, died with angels in his ears and his eyes on Heaven."*

Those three little words threaten to escape about every three minutes, but I hold it together. But fuck all, that is getting tough to do and it has only been two days.

As we pull into my driveway, I am jolted back to the depressing fact that Kris has to go to her own place of residence tonight. In just a few minutes we will part ways and I won't see her until tomorrow, Sunday.

"Tomorrow," I mutter aloud.

"Hm? What's that?" Kris asks from the passenger seat as I put my truck in park. She turns the radio down and unbuckles before turning her face to mine.

"Tomorrow," I say again before clearing my throat. "What are you doing tomorrow? Do you have plans?"

My palms start to sweat, and I don't know why. She is down here *for* me. Why am I so nervous that she might have plans on a Sunday in a place she only knows one person.

"Do I have plans? Here?" Her eyebrows raise and she smiles. "No Carter, I don't have plans tomorrow. Unless we make plans." Kris winks at me and I swear I can feel my blood rush physically pump through my fast beating heart.

I chuckle, trying to shake off the lack of game I am presenting.

"The lake," I suggest as I push my hand through my hair.

It is taking every single atom in my body to hold it together and not bring her perfectly soft lips to mine right now. The moon above us, the stars visible out in this dark country area, the sound of crickets and the motor of an irrigation well a quarter mile south. It all comes together to create one of my favorite things; an evening in the middle of nowhere.

We meet at the driver's side door of her car. She leans back on it and crosses her arms. One foot rests flat against the inside of her calf and I move my gaze from the tips of her black-strapped sandals all the way to the dark lashes of her eyes as I move slowly towards her. I take my time, smiling as I go. She is so fucking beautiful.

And she's really here.

"It still seems unreal that you're here, Kris. That you're real and you're here. For me. With me." I place my hands on her hips, pushing myself closer to her. She moves her foot so that both now touch the concrete. This close she has to look up at me and I will not even pretend that doesn't do something to my ever-loving soul. "I can't believe you're here," I whisper.

"I am," she whispers while fisting the front of my shirt in both of her hands. "And I am so glad that I am, Carter."

I suppress the urge to beg her to say my name until my ears start to fail.

We stay quiet, our foreheads touching.

"The lake, tomorrow. Would you like to come to Ken's cabin and do some fishing and shit tomorrow with me and Kenny?"

Her eyes meet mine and she smiles. "The lake I'm staying by?"

"The one and the same, sweetheart."

"That sounds perfect."

I cannot stop myself now. The smile. The fact that she is so willing to meet my friend and do something that might not be in her norm. The fact that she is here at all. I kiss her. And man, it might very well kill me, kissing this woman.

I'd die happy at least.

"I'll text you when I get to the cabin." Kris is a little breathless and I allow myself to feel good about being responsible for that. "Call me in the morning and I'll meet you there?"

"I'll come pick you up if that's alright?" Hope blooms in my chest.

"That sounds perfect," she says again.

"Perfect," I say, my lips pulling up. "Perfect."

A few more long kisses goodbye and then she is gone. She has taken my entire heart with her, I realize not for the first time today.

Chapter Eleven

Take Your Time

Kris

I barely make it out of Carter's driveway before I have my brother squawking at me on Bluetooth as I go back to my cabin by the lake.

"You will not believe how good my weekend is going, not that you were about to ask," is Bryce's way of greeting.

"I don't think you will believe that Carter has a son," I respond.

"Well, I don't think— wait I'm sorry what?"

"Oh, you heard me. Carter has a son. A whole son, almost three years old, boy, named Cameron. His mother is Carter's best friend, one of them, and they co-parent, from the sounds of it, like an actual dream."

"So," Bryce drawls. "I'm sorry, have you met this boy named Cameron?"

"No, Bryce. I've barely met this man named Carter." My voice is a little harsh. But I feel stressed, and my brother can handle it.

"Let's put all of this aside for a minute. How is it all going?"

"Honestly, Bryce?"

"I always want honesty, Kris."

I inhale deeply and ready myself for the word vomit I am about to spew. I am nothing if not a stress-rambler.

"I know that it sounds insane, and I am probably the last person that would ever condone someone saying what I'm about to say so please know that I don't need you to tell me that this is crazy. I don't need you to tell me that this is so fast and it's so wild and it's so bizarre and it's all of these things. I don't need you to rain on my parade. I just need... you." I exhale.

"You've got me, Kris. Always. Judgment free today."

I can imagine him throwing up the Boy Scouts salute in a way of swearing on the other side of this call.

"I think I love him." I say it quietly but not solemnly.

And I am met with nothing. Silence.

So, I go on. "And not in the 'oh my gosh, I love you so much you're so funny' kind of way. But in the 'I would strip myself bare in negative thirty-degree weather if he needed my shirt' kind of way. 'I would walk over hot coals and physically remove and sell my own kidney' kind of way. 'Give him the last inside piece of the pan of brownies' way, Bryce. 'I'm in love with him and it's fucking terrifying' kind of way."

Bryce gives me nothing aside from a whispered, "But you love the inside part of a pan of brownies."

Which honestly, is fine because I think I just need to talk this out, out loud.

"And I know, like I said, that sounds absolutely insane. Clinically, undeniably, irrevocably crazy. But I also know that I have never felt so *light* in my life."

"What do you mean by light?" His voice is steady but quiet.

I think for a moment on how best to explain this undeniable feeling inside of me. "I have never felt so *free*. So... unburdened and weightless. I have never wanted to just *be* more than I want to *be* with him right now. I have never liked my life in such small minuscule moments the way that I do in the small minuscule moments with Carter."

"So, you're in love with Carter?"

"I am in love with Carter."

"And have you told him that?"

"Well, considering I've spent a total of 12 hours with the man... No, no I have not."

This drive is the perfect drive for a phone call. It's nearly a straight shot to the cabin I am occupying, and the highway is well lit and near empty.

"What do you think he feels?"

"I think that he feels the same way, and I also think that he's nervous about maybe scaring me off."

Bryce scoffs. "Well obviously. You're a fucking flight risk, Kris."

"I am not a flight risk," I defend, even though I feel the lie on my tongue.

Just call me Kris "Flighty" Atwater.

"Kris, I fully supported all of this, and I still support all of this, but I'm telling you right now; you're a flight risk. You went all the way down to Nebraska from North Dakota, on a whim, in search of a man that you met one time five years ago. All because he told you to find him if you ever found yourself in the position to do so. You're the fucking definition of 'flight risk' right now."

"You told me to come down here!" I yell at him, my grip tightening on my steering wheel.

"Yes. Yes, I did. And I'm damn glad you listened."

"Then why are you making it seem like I made a mistake?"

"That's not my intention, I'm sorry. It's just a lot to keep up with and the rational part of my brain is telling me that you are actually crazy. But I would rather you be crazy and genuinely, fully happy for the first time in too long, verses you being rational and sad. Now, I'm not going to talk to you about this anymore. I'm moving on. What are you going to do now?"

I sigh. "Well, tomorrow we're going to the lake."

"The lake that your cabins by?"

"Yes, it's called Harlan Lake. I don't really know what we're doing but I think Carter's friend has a cabin there too and that's who we are going to hang out with."

"So, you're meeting his friends?"

"Well, yes, I would assume that I will be meeting his friend if we're going to his friend's cabin."

"Alright, you're being a little too sassy for me right now. Why don't you take a breath and try again?"

I do as I'm told because he's not wrong. "I'm sorry. The whole flight risk thing stressed me out. I'm a little irritated now."

"I didn't mean it in a negative way. I just meant that I can understand why he would be scared to tell you how he feels in such a direct way."

"Expound."

"Have you told him about you and Michael?" His question is slow and soft.

"Yes."

"Have you told him about the things that happened before you and Michael... ended?"

"Yes, Bryce. I have told him about all of the things that happened before Michael and I split up and then during our divorce."

"So, I think it would be safe to assume that he wants to tread lightly with you so that he doesn't ruin what you've already repaired within yourself."

"Do you think that he thought about that? Watching out for the things that I've already had to fix?"

"Absolutely. I think he's already thought of that. That's the kind of man he seems to be, and I've only met him one time."

"I think this conversation is going to go nowhere other than you telling me to sack up and I'm just not there yet, so I'm going to ask you how wedding planning is going."

"I'm definitely not talking about wedding planning so if your goal is to end this conversation you succeeded."

"I am nothing if not successful."

"A successful pain in my ass. Have you called your mother?"

I needed this change of pace desperately.

"Have you called *your* mother?"

"You need to go to bed. You sound tired," Bryce jokes, poking at my already admitted annoyance.

"And now you sound like mom, so I don't need to call her." I sigh. "No, I haven't called her, not today. I will call her tomorrow morning while I wait for Carter to come pick me up."

"Well, I would refrain from telling her that you're madly and deeply in love with a man you've only known for a day, because Lord only knows what kind of shit she'll come up with and honestly, I wouldn't put it past the woman to drive down there herself just to meet him."

"That's a frightening and realistic thought. I will be keeping that to myself. Good call."

"Kris," Bryce says slowly. "I love you."

I breathe deeply and exhale, letting myself relax.

"Yeah, I love you too. Say hi to the Sher for me."

"Hey, when are you coming back?"

"I don't really know. I haven't thought that far ahead."

Bryce chokes on a laugh. "Who are you and what have you done with my sister?"

"Har har." I roll my eyes even though he can't see it. "I'll talk to you later, I love you."

"Love you too. Bye."

After hanging up with my brother, it only takes me about ten more minutes to get back to the cabin. I park in the little gravel driveway that is next to my cabin before going inside. The AC works so well in here, so automatically I am ready to get into my comfy sweatpants and a shittier t-shirt. I can't wait to take my bra off, wash my face and just settle down for a little while. These last two days have caught up with me, I think.

I am most certainly not feeling any sort of negativity towards the events that have transpired, but it is a lot to take in. It's a lot emotionally and it's a lot to think about and a lot to maybe question.

Carter. Nebraska. Cameron.

I set down my purse and my keys on the table next to the door as I walk inside, flipping off my sandals behind the brown couch. Before I do anything, I remember to plug my phone in to charge in the kitchen. I go through the living room and down the hall, into the bathroom where I have my pajamas and my face wash. I go about my business, feeling a little less frazzled with a clean face and freed boobs.

I look up into the mirror and force myself into a staring contest.

"We're having a come to Jesus moment, you and I," I say to myself. *Out loud.*

Might as well just own the fact that I think I am insane.

"We need to talk about what we are doing here exactly."

I stop talking aloud but keep the inner monologue going.

What is the game plan? It is early and everything but there is something real between us and I think that I want to give that a shot. But how do I know where he stands and what about his son?

The last thing that I would want is for Carter and me to get close and eventually get to the point where I meet Cameron, but then something shifts, or something happens, or something changes because life does that. Life fucks you up sometimes. And I do not want somebody who doesn't even have the choice to be in the crossfire, caught in a situation where things might go bad. So, now I am not only thinking about myself, I am not only thinking of Carter, but I am thinking about a probably sweet two-year-old boy. I do not ever want to be the kind of person that ruins something for someone's child. A failed relationship when a kid is involved can affect everyone, not just the adults. I had resigned to the fact that it was just going to be me, that Michael thought I was broken and so I must have been. That my body decided that it just does not want to have kids and so I am just not going to. I accepted and dealt with all of the stuff and now all of a sudden, I am kind of in love with this man I do not even know. And he has his own child. And I do not know where that puts me.

I hang up the sandy colored hand towel on the bright silver hook next to the sink. I take one last look in the mirror while I let out a big breath.

It has only been two days, I am paid up for a month in this cabin. In the grand scheme of things there is no rush. I decide I am going to take it day by day. It is not a big deal until it needs to be a big deal and I do not have to make a plan right now because I am, at the end of the day, the only person I am responsible for *right now.*

I nod at myself in the mirror before I turn around, shut off the light and go to my phone.

I will not admit it aloud, but I am hoping slightly that there is a text from a certain farmer thirty minutes north. When I pick up my phone, I see a text from the aforementioned farmer and smile.

Please let me know you are home safe.

Yes, I'm sorry I didn't text when I got here. I got home probably 15 minutes ago and decided to wash my face and get ready for bed. I'm safe and sound and nice and cool in my very air-conditioned cabin.

No worries. I just wanted to make sure you got there and didn't forget to let me know. I would've had to drive down there and look for you if I hadn't heard back eventually Glad you're home safe I can't wait to see you in the morning.

I smile at my phone, thinking the very same thing.

Call me when you're on your way xoxo

Good night sweetheart.

I grab my charger from the wall, sliding my phone into the pocket of my brown sweatpants. I fill up my purple Simple Modern Trek and take a long drink of water. After hauling everything to my room and putting it all where it goes, I crawl under the big comforter, pulling it up to my chin and straightening it out. Then I pray to God that he helps guide me through this insane time in my life, and that I do not end up crawling through the pits of rock bottom once again.

Really scraped up my knees the last time. Those wounds healed though; *I am okay.*

Chapter Twelve

The Lakes

Kris

Morning was here before I even knew it. I am standing with my butt leaned up against the counter of the kitchen, a pair of black leggings and a loose, white Taylor Swift eras concert T-shirt on. I washed my hair this morning, so I have got that down and air drying. Nebraska's humidity would have messed it all up even if I had tried to blow it dry. So, half frizzy and half damp is the look we are getting today. After a couple days of no make-up, because I didn't really see a point in trying to impress the man with a façade like that, I decided that since I am about to meet Carter's friend, I better put on at least something that will make me feel like I look a little more presentable. Tinted moisturizer and some mascara, very minimal blush and a light pink lip stain are the best anyone around here is going to get from me right now because it is one-hundred fucking degrees at nine in the morning and I am questioning why anyone chooses to live in southern Nebraska during the summer.

I hear a soft knock on the door before it opens slowly and I see Carter's head pop in. I hum happily that he listened to my text this morning where I told him to let himself in, after I woke up and unlocked the door. I smile automatically, without thought, but stay put in the kitchen waiting for him to walk in. I don't have to wait long before he is striding across the trailer for where I'm standing.

It is almost animalistic. And it is most certainly hot.

Carter is grabbing my face with his hands in the next breath. They are rough and smooth, warm and cool, strong and sturdy. My stomach feels like a million little butterflies have taken flight and my breath hitches just slightly. I look up into his eyes before his lips touch mine, and I catalog this moment as one of those very small minuscule moments. The kind that keeps me grounded when I feel as if I could just simply float away.

"Good morning, darling."

Gosh, his voice.

Carter steps back one step looking to see what is in my mug.

"You got any coffee in there with that creamer?" His smile is taunting, teasing.

"Nope, I don't drink the stuff. Just straight milky sugar for me," I joke back.

I take a long sip and wink at Carter over my bright yellow mug. He laughs and it is the sweetest sound I have ever heard.

He looks around for the coffee pot, his melodic laugh still echoing in my brain, before going to pour his own cup.

His gaze doesn't leave mine from across the kitchen as he takes his first sip. "Oh, at least she makes good coffee."

"Been practicing since I was sixteen," I laugh.

"How did you sleep out here last night, sweetheart?"

Fucking hell. I am one "sweetheart" away from changing my address.

"I actually didn't sleep bad which is kind of surprising. I've traveled somewhat often throughout my life, and I've always been like, a fine sleeper wherever I go. But never a great sleeper. For some reason, though, I didn't have any troubles here. I don't know if it's the sound of the water that I can't really hear through the walls," I laugh at my own joke. "Or if it's the fact that I've just been so busy the last couple days and by the time I laid my head down I was just ready for sleep, but I slept really well."

That was the longest answer to a single question in the history of answers.

"I'm so glad to hear that Nebraska's agreeing with you as much as I am."

I feel my cheeks warm, and I smile slightly as I take another drink of my coffee.

"Ken says we can head over whenever," Carter slides his phone back into his front jeans pocket. "So, just let me know when you're ready and we can head out."

"I'm ready now." I step away from the counter. "I can put these in a couple to-go cups if you want."

"Yeah, that would be great."

The cabin is fully furnished with cups and utensils and anything else that you would need for a lake weekend. Other than food and the coffee grounds themselves, the place came stocked. I walk over to where I already had found the to-go cups, they're the cardboard ones that you would get at a coffee shop. Perfect for today.

"Do I need a hat or anything for where we're going, or what we are doing?"

"Do you have a hat?" Carter asks incredulously.

"Well, no," I drawl out. "I guess I don't." I laugh at myself.

"I've got one in my pickup," he says with a smile.

Carter gets to the passenger door first and opens it for me. After hoisting myself up and setting my drink in one of the empty cupholders I turn to close my still open door and catch him staring at me.

I put my hands under my thighs, my stomach feeling fluttery, and ask him, "Something the matter?"

He smiles at me, his big, beautiful smile and shakes his head. "Nope, everything's perfect."

He reaches for my hand and kisses my knuckles before setting it back down gently and closing the door.

Small minuscule moment seventy-three... perfection.

"So," I say slowly. "I'm kind of nervous to meet your friend."

"Oh no, don't be. It's just Ken. He's the chill-est. He was at that concert with me when I first met you."

"Oh gosh," I mutter. Suddenly even more nervous. "So, I don't want to know what he probably thinks about this whole situation then, huh?"

Carter just laughs and shakes his head. "Ken has only ever wanted to see me be happy. He is actually ecstatic. He's excited to meet you and hang out today."

Ken's cabin is only five minutes away from the one that I am staying at. It is a relatively similar double-wide trailer. Brown gravel driveway, a tattered once-was white awning over a red wood porch. There is lawn furniture sprinkled throughout the yard and on the porch. A sliding glass door puts you into the living room and kitchen. Very basic, very cute, very homey.

"Honey. I'm home," Carter calls out as he closes the door.

"Well, darling, is that you?" Ken, I assume, yells back in a faux southern accent.

I laugh quietly to myself as I sip on my coffee.

"Baby, honey, sugar pie. Come give me some loving." Carter starts to head down the hall that leads to what I am guessing are the bedrooms.

"Don't have to tell me twice." Ken's voice is closer now and far more Nebraskan.

The next thing I know a six foot four, blonde, tan and lean man barrels through the hallway before wrapping his arms around Carter's waist. Ken picks Carter up and then goes to throw him down on the couch before stopping and just setting him back on his feet, bracing his hands on Carter's shoulders.

"Man, I feel like I haven't seen you in days."

"Ken, I just saw you two days ago." Carter laughs.

My eyes flit between the two of them as I stay near the entryway and caffeinate.

"I would like it noted that that *is* multiple days," Ken points out.

"You're very clingy."

Ken ignores Carter and turns to me. "Who's this pretty young lady?"

"Ken, this is Kris. Kris, this is Ken."

I smile from where I'm standing, giving a small but enthusiastic wave.

"Don't be too much, but don't be weird about it," I tell myself.

"I know it's been five years, but I'd recognize you anywhere I think."

His comment catches me off guard and I laugh, not knowing what to say to that. I look around at his cabin and mention how much I like it.

"Thanks. It's a good bachelor pad. Are you having a nice vacation down here?"

Ken goes to his kitchen and picks up his own coffee mug. I notice Carter's shoulders tense just a little bit before he shakes it off like it was nothing. I'm not sure, but I am wondering if maybe the term "vacation" is a little too loose for his liking. I cannot honestly say that I would disagree.

"I am having a really nice time. It's only been a couple of days but the cabin I'm staying at is great and tagging along to work with Carter yesterday was really fun."

Ken wiggles his eyebrows at me and says, "Oh I bet it was."

I blush and laugh. Then I watch as Carter walks up behind Ken and slaps him on the back of the head as he tells him to mind his manners.

Ken runs his hand over the spot Carter just smacked and says, "All in good fun, buddy."

I hear Carter mutter something under his breath. It sounded an awful lot like "good fun my ass", so I just smile into my coffee. Carter walks over to a bowl of green grapes that are sitting on the kitchen counter and starts eating them.

"So, what are we doing today kids?" Ken asks us.

"Well Ken, you invited us over. So why don't you tell me, bud?"

"Oh, well shoot." Ken grabs the back of his neck. "I didn't have anything concrete planned, but I was thinking that maybe we could take the boat out and go fishing. Have you fished before?" he asks me.

"Oh yeah, I love fishing. That's one of my family's favorite things to do up in North Dakota."

"Oh, great!" Ken steps forward. "We can get you a fishing license online and then just go from there."

"Yeah, that sounds perfect."

I take my phone out of the pocket of my leggings. I get the website pulled up and start putting my information in. Carter walks over and takes my phone right out of my hands before I get very far. My bright pink phone case looks so small and out of place in his large, tan hand.

"If you put in your info, I want to get your license for you."

I laugh and go to grab my phone back and he pulls it away, raising his arm higher so it's out of reach.

"Carter," I say sternly with an amused smile on my face. "That's okay, I can handle my own fishing license."

Carter closes the distance between us and brings my phone down. "I know you can handle it sweetheart, but I would like to get it for you anyways."

I roll my eyes, already knowing that I cannot really win a situation like this without throwing an unnecessary fit. Not that I honestly want to because I think it is very sweet that he wants to buy it for me.

"Fine." I cross my arms over my chest. "But when I out-fish you later today, you need to remember that you did this to yourself."

His smile grows and he hands me my phone back to enter my information.

"I can't wait to see that."

It didn't take long for Ken and Carter to load up everything that we needed to go fishing. His boat was already on a trailer, hooked up to the back of his pickup. All we have to do was pile into the cab of it and drive a couple miles to the boat ramp.

Watching the two of them work together to get the boat into the water was like watching a well-oiled machine. I could tell that they have done this a time or two.

It's a quiet ride as far as talking goes on our way out to the spot that Ken wants to fish at. The motor was too loud to not have to yell over. The mist from the lake and the wind from the drive is all so nostalgic. Suddenly I am struck with a little bit of homesickness. Not enough to dampen my mood though.

But I do miss North Dakota. Or rather, my family. I miss Sherry's baking and cheery southern laughter. I miss Bryce's scowl. My mom and dad, I miss their yammering.

The sun is hot and high in the sky and as I look around, I take note of how busy it is down here.

"Is this a pretty busy lake normally?" I ask, speaking into Carter's ear so I don't have to scream.

I feel him shiver and let myself believe it was me that caused it.

"Oh yeah, this is a popular place to fish and swim."

I doubt he misses the same shiver he gives me when he speaks that into my own ear.

"It's one of the only places in this general area to do this kind of recreational stuff at."

"Yeah," I hum. "It's so beautiful down here. I love it."

Ken's voice and the sudden quiet interrupts the moment of eye contact I was savoring as he asks, "I think we'll just troll for a little while. Is that all right?"

"I'm good with that," Carter says while I nod my head.

Once our hooks are in the water and all of us are just kind of posted up around the boat in our specific spot's, things just slow down. I find myself mentally taking stock once again. Not in such a panicked way as I was last night, but more in just a mental checklist sort of way.

"What are you thinking about over there, Kris?"

I laugh at Ken's question, watching the glare Carter throws at him while he casts his line again.

I lock eyes with Carter while I say, "I was just thinking about the last couple of days and how much fun I've had."

"He's a good time, huh?" Ken asks, his tone not *at all* suggestive.

I laugh again.

Gosh, I think I have laughed more in the couple days that I have been here than I have in the last several years. That fact is not lost on me.

Carter doesn't laugh but he does roll his eyes in amusement.

I listen while the both of them talk about their work weeks—everything they have scheduled so far. I learn that Ken works for a co-op in town as a salesman and so this time of year gets pretty busy for him too, just like it does for Carter, with harvest coming up. We all talk about our fishing stories that we have had over the years. I laugh when Carter and Ken gripe to each other about their "big fish" stories and how the other ones lying about how big it was. I can't help but feel a little homesick again when I think about my brother and I and how the banter is similar between us. We talk about our families, and I tell them about Bryce and Sherry, and my parents. I learn that Carter doesn't have any other family members that he is in close contact with, none in an immediate capacity. I learn Ken's got six siblings and I can't help but be a little shocked, but then at the same time it also makes complete sense. His comedic genius, the way he teases and plays, is definitely something he seems to have come by naturally.

The afternoon goes by quickly. None of us catch a single thing. Fishing today though, had become the bottom priority. The talking and stories and laughing took first spot and I enjoyed the whole thing immensely.

"What do you say we head back and grill up some hotdogs and have a couple drinks before we call it a night? Tomorrow's Monday and I know I've got an early morning."

Carter nods in agreement and I mention how I have got an early conference call in the morning.

I lean into Carter as we head back to the dock, his arm around my shoulders tightly. I look up at him as he faces forward. I know he knows, and I do not know why but I feel zero shame as I blatantly ogle him anyways.

The sun is still up and shining brightly, now dipping down a little in the west. The light is more golden and the way Carter's already tan skin glows in it...

"You're beautiful," I say almost accidentally.

He turns his gaze to meet mine and smiles as he places a small kiss on my brow.

We stay like that, his lips on my forehead and a permanent smile etched onto my mouth. My hand moves to find his, placing both on the top of his leg. I close my eyes and soak it all in. I lock in the smell of the water off the lake and the same minty-tobacco scent that has become Carter to me.

After a minute in that position, I lift my mouth and press my lips to his.

"Thank you," he says against me.

"Thank *you*," I say back.

I feel Ken's eyes on us, and I note that I don't feel even an ounce of embarrassment in this moment. Just... Happiness. Quiet, peaceful, happiness.

Chapter Thirteen

I Think About You

Carter

I've got Cameron for the next couple of days, and I am already missing Kris. Not in a way that is taking away from time with my kid, never that. But in the same way I miss Cameron when he is not with me. It's like this ache in my chest that is almost bittersweet.

"Cameron-Cameron," I holler from the kitchen. "Supper time, bud."

I hear his little feet on the floor as he runs from the couch where he was watching Blippi on Netflix.

"Set the table, kid." I hand Cameron the forks and napkins for tonight. Two of each, like always. But tonight, my fingers almost itch to grab a third.

I definitely do not want to rush Kris, and I am not a "can we skip to the good part" kind of guy because what about everything in between? However, I would be lying if I said I'm not wishing very slightly that we could skip ahead a little bit so that I could introduce my woman to my boy.

Alas, we are reasonable and responsible adults around here and I would not want Cameron meeting a man his mom is with too soon, so here we are.

"Spaggie!" Cameron squeals as I set his little plastic blue plate in front of him.

Someday he will say it the correct way and I honestly dread that moment. So, I don't correct him about it being "spaghetti". Instead, I soak in the youth and charm that is my kid.

"You bet, Cam. Spaggie night. And bath night."

Cameron wastes no time digging in. He has a big appetite with his big personality. Being only two, Cam won't fully grasp anything about what is going on with Kris. Regardless, I don't like to feel like I am keeping something from him so I bring it up during supper.

"So, kiddo. I've got a new friend. She's really nice and I think you might like her a lot. She's kind of like Lance, only she's my friend and not just mama's."

"New fend?"

"Yeah, bud. Her name is Kris and she's really nice."

"She like spaggie?"

I chuckle. "You know what, I don't know. I'll ask her when I talk to her later and let you know. Sound good?"

"Soun good," he says around a mouth full of noodles and sauce.

We go about our night per usual. It looks like he got more sauce *on* him than *in* him. The same can be said about the bath water and the lack of containment in the tub. Before I know it, he is in his Paw Patrol pajamas and tucked into his little twin sized bed. His John Deere comforter is pulled clear up to his chin and he has been read his book, *You're My Little Cuddle Bug*. I brush my hand over his forehead and bend down to give him a kiss.

"I love you buddy."

"Luh you dad. Seet deems."

"Sweet dreams Cameron." One more kiss to his little nose and I'm out the door, smiling like I do every night after our bedtime routine.

I put supper away and clean the kitchen up before changing into my grey sweats and turning on *Friends With Benefits* for some background noise. Then I grab my cellphone and click on Kris' name to FaceTime her.

Thank God she's an iPhone girl.

That way when— no. If she ever leaves, I won't have to go days without laying eyes on her.

Do I sound stalkery? Yes. But listen... I *am* obsessed. And I don't know that I really mind sounding insane all that much.

"Hey, you," she says with a small smile.

Bare face full of freckles, dark hair pulled up to the top of her head in a mess of a bun, light brown sweater over a dark gray t-shirt. This one has some sort of rock and roll band on it, I think. *"Manon and the Blackbeacks"?* Never heard of them, but the shirt looks cool. Her sparkly-black glasses are sitting on the tip of her nose. I want to reach in and push them up for her.

"Hey, you," I say back after what is probably too much time spent ogling. "How was your day?"

She yawns before saying, "it was good. I got a lot of work done. Had some calls this morning and then just spent the day between working outside on the deck to working in here on the couch. It was really nice, actually. Peaceful and productive. Watched a lot of people come in and out through the day. Boats and skis and coolers, galore." Her cheeks get a little rosy and her eyes roll. "And that was the longest answer to that question."

I laugh and shake my head. "I would have kept listening."

She shakes her head and bites her bottom lip. "How was your day? How's Cameron?"

The fact that she asks about Cameron should not be this monumentally incredible, but it is anyways.

"My day was good. Cows are good, corn is good. Cameron is great. He had an awesome weekend with Sadie and her boyfriend. Had a good day at daycare. They include some preschool stuff into their day-to-day schedule at this place, and today he came home knowing how to count to twelve." I shake my head and run my hand over my mouth. "I was floored. I swear it's like he's sixteen all of a sudden."

"That sounds very cool!"

Kris says it with such enthusiasm, it feels so genuine. The excitement over something that most would find not *that* awesome.

I smile, feeling proud of my kid. "It is very cool."

We sit there, just watching each other for a moment.

"Hey," I start, "I kind of missed you today."

She smiles bashfully. "I kind of missed you too, Carter."

My smile grows. "So, listen."

"Fully listening."

I chuckle. "I don't know if you're a football fan but in Nebraska, you kind of have to be." I am sure she thinks I'm kidding... But I'm almost not. "And it's about that time of the year. There's a home game in Lincoln in a month. I was thinking I could take you? You could experience the whole Memorial Stadium thing. You don't even really have to like football or the Huskers to enjoy a Husker game. The whole day is just kind of wild and cool and fun and-"

"I'd love to go to a game with you, honey."

Her smile is soft, and her eyes are crinkled with amusement. My rambling was sending me into a spiral and my heart is beating a million miles a minute. I take a deep breath and release it on a laugh.

"You'll go?"

"I'll go." She nods and smiles at me.

"Great," I say. "Awesome."

In my head I am thinking "that means she'll still be here in a month" but I'm trying to not scare her out of Nebraska, so I'm still attempting to play it cool.

"Tell me about your family."

She sits back on the couch she's on, pulling her sweater up more on her shoulders. Her now purple fingernails glint as she pushes her glasses up with her index finger.

"Gosh, okay," she sighs. "My family. I don't remember what all we talked about yesterday, so I'll start from the beginning I suppose. Well, I have one brother. You met Bryce, kind of, at the concert in

South Dakota. He's got a fiancé, Sherry. They are both incredible. My best friends. Bryce manages a grocery store and Sherry teaches second grade. They're great together. He's high-strung sometimes but she's so calm usually. Very Yin and Yang. And then my mom and dad are great. Penny and John. My mom has always stayed home. With us when we were kids obviously, and then just making the home what it is after we started getting older. She volunteers a ton for local organizations and runs lots of councils for random things. It's honestly hard to keep track of everything she's involved in. She can be a lot but she's great. And then my dad owns a heating and air business. Atwater Heating and Air. You'd think that would mean I might know something about any of that, but I don't."

Kris laughs and starts playing with a piece of her dark hair that has freed itself from the pink scrunchie holding the rest hostage. And like the moment with her glasses earlier, I want to reach in and take the scrunchie out of her hair and watch it all fall around her face. I refocus on her words as she continues.

"It was never my thing to go to work with dad and pay attention to whatever he was doing. They're both great too though. Honest and kind and funny. Very North Dakotan."

The way her accent comes out more the further in to her story makes me smile even wider. I'm obsessed with way she says things like "Dakotan" and "go". She takes a break and smiles softly, like she's missing them. I'm sure she is. An ache takes place in my gut over the thought.

"I've got a pretty big extended family. Lots of aunts and uncles and cousins. They are all over the states though. Get togethers are usually every couple of years and really large. There's one coming up in May actually. This one's at a lake in North Dakota so we don't have to go far but sometimes they are in Iowa. One time we all went to Nashville. That was wild." Her laugh flits through my ears, through my heart.

"They all sound incredible." I smile and mean it. But I cannot help the small twinge of envy I feel.

I've got Cameron. And Ken and Sadie, and then Lance in a way. But that's really it. My parents have been gone for so long and they did not come from very large or close families. I have sometimes wondered what it would be like to have more people that love me—that love Cameron.

"They are." Kris's smile gets sad. "And you?" Her question is coated in caution.

"Well, biologically it's Cameron. Everyone else is gone, or I'm not familiar with them. But then I have Ken. And Sadie. They're my family and they're great. You met Ken, obviously. Sadie is really good too. She's the mother of my son but beyond that she's one of my champions." I smile, thinking about the way we got here. "We had a weird start, but I can't really imagine my life without her. It's all platonic now, no doubt. She's got a good boyfriend that's great to Cameron and her family is a couple hours in every direction, so Cameron's got a really great support system around him on that side. That's really it, though, for me. Small but good. Whole."

"Ken is really fun. I loved spending the day with him and you yesterday. Sadie sounds incredible. I hope to meet her sometime."

And I believe her.

"Yeah, she'd love that." I don't want to scare her off, but fuck this round about bull shit. "So, listen. At risk of freaking you out," I see her face get serious. "I don't want to pressure you into meeting Cameron just yet." She visibly relaxes and I laugh. "But I think it might be cool if you met Sadie?" I suggest.

"Oh," she exhales and smiles. "I think that would actually be super nice. It would stress me out to eventually meet Cameron before his mom. Like, for her, that can't be an easy kind of thing."

She's so fucking thoughtful.

"I'll talk with her tomorrow. I pick Cameron up on Tuesdays for her and bring him to her house after him and I get ice cream."

"I love your little routines with him."

"It's easy that it's just me and him, I'm lucky there."

We go through some more small talk. Favorite television shows, movies, bands. I ask about "Manon and the Blackbeaks" on her shirt and am quickly schooled when she explains that it is this whole thing from a book series. Something about fire and magic, "witchling's" and "princeling's". I love that she reads. Makes me feel smart just knowing her.

Before I know it, we have been FaceTiming for an hour and a half. Her small yawn and heavy eyelids are the only thing that makes me check the time.

"Bedtime, sweetheart."

She smiles at me and nods. "I know but I was really enjoying talking to you."

"Well, we can do it again tomorrow."

"It's a date," she says and my heart stutters. "Goodnight Carter."

"Goodnight, Kris."

Fucking hell. An hour and a half, and it was not nearly enough. I am wired and ready to go. I want to call her back and demand we just set the phones on our pillows and talk until one of us falls asleep. But we are not seventeen and I don't know if that is cute or weird at our age.

So, I go to bed. Phone plugged in and on my little brown bedside table. Kris Atwater does not leave my mind for even a second.

Chapter Fourteen

Hail Varsity

Kris

"No, Sherry. I will not *accidentally* forget to pack pajamas." I scoff at my almost-sister-in-law. More best friend than that though.

"Why?! Give me one good reason why you refuse to pick up the damn pace with Farm Daddy? This would be the perfect opportunity. You're going away for the weekend with him. Staying at a hotel overnight. Kris. Come. On."

I laugh and shake my head. "Farm Daddy, Sher? Are you serious?"

"Tell me you hate it, honestly." She rolls her eyes, knowing already that I love it.

"I might put him in my phone as that," I say more to myself. *Farm Daddy is absolutely a thing now.*

We both laugh at ourselves.

"Sherry, I'm not pushing things or rushing shit. It's been such a good month, and the pace has definitely contributed to that. So please, for the love of me and my pajamas, relax girlfriend."

"Yes, fine fine. I will stop. But-"

"Nope," I cut her off. "No buts. You and Bryce both are so dang pushy." I laugh again.

"We just love you and want you to be happy."

I say the last bit at the same time as her and she glares at me.

"I know. I love you. I have to finish packing. I'll Snapchat you while we're there. Sounds like this is a very big deal around here."

"Okay, okay. I love you. Call me and stuff. Bye babe."

Upon hanging up, I immediately change Carter's name to *Farm Daddy* in my phone and giggle.

This last month really has been a dream.

We have spent the weekends that Cameron has been with Sadie together. During the week we kept it so casual and light, making time to see each other but not pushing ourselves to exhaustion to make it happen. The days we didn't see each other we would FaceTime at night before bed for at least an hour. He FaceTimed my parents with me one night when he was at the cabin that I have started calling home. Little dates here and there but mostly one of us cooks and we just sit and talk. Go for walks. Hang out with Ken. I have plans with Sadie and Carter on Wednesday to get lunch while Cameron is at daycare. I'm nervous but more excited than anything to meet her and start the process of getting us all ready for me to meet sweet Cameron.

The game tonight is in Lincoln, and it is an evening game. It will go pretty late so Carter got us a hotel room at a place downtown that apparently, and I quote, "has the best mother fucking omelet bar you will ever experience." I am going to go to his place, and he will take us from there. Ken is meeting us in Lincoln and staying with one of his "lady friends". I am beyond looking forward to the whole thing.

The hotel situation, I admit, I am a little nervous for. Carter got two queen beds because I told him two rooms was insane. We are adults. We can share a room and be just fine.

But I don't know if I can be just fine in a room with him. He's so good. I mean...

So good.

We have kept things fairly above board. Or above clothes. Not totally though, and when I say that the self-control we both have going for us is damn near herculean, I'm not being dramatic.

So. Good.

I will not be accidentally forgetting my pajamas in this little duffel bag I am zipping up. But I also will not be grabbing my standard granny panties that I sleep in at night either. Happy medium. You know, just in case.

As I go to walk out the door, slipping on my white sneakers, I take a last look in the mirror. I tried today. Like, *tried tried.*

I have on some black leggings— comfort is key. An oversized white Nebraska Huskers long-sleeve shirt. My hair is perfectly curled and texturized and half of it is pulled back into a bright red clip. My eyes are shadowed in a sparkly rose gold and my eyelashes are having the best mascara day. My bronzer is bronzing, and my blush is blushing. I channeled Taylor Swift as I put on my favorite bright red lip-stain.

Lip-stain!

I spin around and run into the bathroom to grab my red lip-stain and take a breath.

If that is not the most dramatic reaction to almost forgetting a lip product... I take another deep breath before moving my feet again.

Relax, Kris. It is fine. He is a man, and you are a woman. And he likes you and you lo— like him. You like him. And he's handsome and funny and sweet and smart and the way he looks at you only makes your knees slightly weak, and you are so royally fucked in the heart.

My pep-talk only makes me want to vomit. So, I stop by the door and close my eyes, setting everything down and shaking out my hands.

"Enough, you psycho. You are freaking out and for what? He is a good man. You are not so bad either. It is fine. It will be what it will be. And it will all be fine."

I should get "fine" tattooed on my forehead.

This round of crazy does the trick and I breathe easy now.

It is all okay. And if shit gets frisky tonight, then that is alright by me too.

Lincoln, Nebraska on a home game day is unreal. I am so far out of my element in the best way.

The Sea of Red is not an exaggeration. I swear this place would show up on a picture from the moon.

It is loud and beautiful outside. The people are nice, and the stadium is "dry" so everyone is either sober or sobering up as the evening goes by. We got here early and tailgated with the company Carter buys his corn seed from. He held my hand the entire time and introduced me as his girlfriend to everyone we met. I might have been imagining it, but the prideful tone of his voice made my knees a little weak.

We are at our seats now, they're right on the forty-yard line and nearly front row, so we can see *everything*.

I am looking around, taking it all in. The red and white on everyone's shirts. The yellow corncob hats a few people are toting around. The air is crisp, and the vibe is fun.

"Incredible, isn't it?"

Carter's question sweeps across my cheek as he leans in to ask it. It's not loud enough to not be able to simply talk but I truly do not mind the closeness. He has been like this all day. Near. It is as if he simply can't help himself. Like his being right next to me, touching me, is unstoppable and the itch to feel me cannot be scratched; a kiss on the cheek, a hand on my back, linking arms... I love it.

I turn, our eyes locking and our noses brushing. "It's perfect."

He leans in the rest of the way and kisses me. Kisses me probably too earnestly for a football stadium but I don't say anything. How could I when he's consuming my breath, my thoughts, my soul. I kiss him back. I match him. His hands rest on my hips, fisting my shirt, pulling me closer to him. I slide my hands up his strong arms and over his broad shoulders. I frame his face, resting them on his stubbled cheeks, running my thumbs over the dark scruff.

"Do you ever grow this out?" I ask as he rests his lips on my brow.

"It's been a while." His mouth doesn't leave my skin.

I hum in response.

"Think I should, sweetheart?"

I nod against his chest, lightly, so as not to disturb the makeup I carefully applied today. "Absolutely would not complain about a beard, baby."

He pauses mid chuckle, his chest no longer vibrating against me.

I look up and meet his darkened blue eyes.

"I'm torn between begging you to call me that all the time, and also pleading for you to not call me that again until I can get us to a place of privacy." His voice is deeper than usual and rasps through the air between us. The air that is now plenty charged.

I swallow, blinking my wide eyes at Carter. "Noted," I say quietly, and a little too breathy.

I feel like the sun is beating down on me with how hot I just got.

He kisses me, this time quickly, and we turn our attention back to our surroundings.

The game is going well, and the crowd is rowdy. We had Valentino's pizza after the first quarter. Ken met us at halftime at our seats to say hi. He did not bring his "friend" he came with, and I told him I was bummed. He laughed but did not divulge from there, so I let it go. I made a mental note to bug Carter about it later though.

I love a good cup of hot tea.

As the game's clock winds down and the score is set at a tie, Nebraska takes their places for their last play and the atmosphere is intense. I have never ever felt anything like it before.

You truly do not have to be a football fan, or a Nebraska fan, to enjoy a game day at Memorial Stadium.

The ball makes it into the end zone at the last second and the Huskers win by a hair and a good play. I feel like the whole state just shook with cheers. Everyone is high-fiving and hugging and jumping up and down. Someone a few rows above us yells "GO BIG RED!" and I join in, not for the first time tonight, in the responding, slower "GO! BIG! RED!"

Even as we walk to the hotel, the vibes stick with us. The hotel is near the stadium and apparently everyone else's is too. We are a traveling Sea of Red at this point.

"I want to do this again. Whenever. Every year. That was incredible!" I grab the front of Carter's black hoodie and give him a light shake. His laugh settles into my heart and into my soul.

I'm so far gone.

"We can absolutely make that happen, sweetheart." Carter wraps his hands around the backs of my elbows, running them up and down from there to my shoulders.

We are waiting at a crosswalk, dozens, if not hundreds of people around us. The light turns and people are walking around us and it feels like I am in a movie. Strangers everywhere. Children on their dad's shoulders chanting small "go big red's". Mom's laughing and shaking their heads while they try to zip up little jackets as the nighttime air gets chilly. Small groups of friends hanging on each other's shoulders and laughing about something called "Elk Creek Water". A whole world is walking around us, buzzing about and living, thriving. But for me there is only the handsome man in my grasp. I should feel embarrassed or ashamed or bashful or something equally off-kilter. I don't though. Not in the slightest. I feel confident and comfortable and excited. I seize this moment, not giving a single fuck about what is going on around us. I stand on my toes and bring my lips to his, pulling him close. Like, *really* close. And I kiss the life into him. I let him kiss the life back into me. The life that dimmed— that died along with dreams and a marriage that feels decades old by now. I kiss this man. This man that I know I love, but feel like I perhaps shouldn't already.

Our kissing stops but our bodies stay locked together. It's just us on this street corner, but I have never felt less alone.

"Hotel?" Carter asks, breathless and gruffly.

"Hotel, baby," I say with zero hesitation and probably too much enthusiasm.

He makes a noise that is half chuckle and half groan against my mouth, and I eat it up, letting him fill my body with that sound.

And then we seize that night. We seize that feeling and that love and that passion and that light. We use the second bed in our room as a suitcase holder and nothing more.

And the next morning I experience "the best mother fucking omelet bar of my life".

Chapter Fifteen

September

Carter

It is the middle of the day, on a Wednesday, in September and the weather is feeling like fall. The corn is looking nice and dead, ready to be picked. Soybeans are about to start falling so they are ready to be cut. I might take the combine out tomorrow and get started if things are dry enough. I make a mental note to take some samples to the local co-op for moisture testing.

I park my pickup at the restaurant in Alma. It's a small pizza shop that has the best cheese sticks, and I'm looking forward to those and a glass of ice-cold tea. It is like my eyes know exactly where Kris is at because as I step into the building, they immediately land on her. Her dark hair is down and curled slightly, and my fingers itch to tangle themselves in between each strand. To free the half that is up in a little pearl clip and turn her gaze to me. Her brown sweater, that I have come to learn is one of three in extremely similar shades, covers what I know on a very personal level now to be a fine as hell ass in black leggings. I do not care who sees me right now as I stop to check out my girl. To watch as she flips the little white plastic menu between her loving hands.

Back and forth, side one and side two, over and over.

My smile grows.

She's nervous. Even though I have told her several times that Sadie is probably more excited to make Kris her new best friend than anything else, she's still been a little anxious. But Kris did tell me how serious she is taking this, and it honestly warmed my heart a bit. So I won't make fun of her for being a little ball of worry.

"You don't need to be nervous, sweetheart," I say quietly as I take the seat next to her. I press a kiss to the top of her head and breathe her in. *Vanilla and mint.* "Sadie is more excited to make you her new shopping partner than anything."

I laugh but Kris doesn't.

Now I'm starting to worry. "You okay, Kris?"

She looks at me, chewing on the inside of her lip. I run a hand down her back, the sweater catching ever so slightly on the rough callouses on my palm.

"What if she hates me and doesn't ever want me to meet Cameron and then we have to stop whatever it is we're doing, and this is all just a big mistake?"

I take a breath to stop myself from laughing because I may not know much about women, but I do know laughing at them when they are worried is not smart.

"You're going to chew a hole through your lip if you don't stop worrying so much, sweetheart." I run my thumb over her mouth, and she closes her eyes. I kiss the tip of her nose before sitting back. "We'll talk about the whole 'whatever it is we're doing' part later. When we are alone and I can show you exactly what it is we are doing here and how I intend to be doing that for the rest of my life." Her eyes widen and her mouth pops open on a small gasp. I take great pride in both of those responses. "But for now, sweetheart, relax please. I know Sadie and I know you. And I know for a fact that she will love you, but at the very least she will approve of you knowing Cameron. It's going to be fine. It's not an interview. You're not going in for any sort of trial. You're wonderful. Sadie already knows that." I smile and frame her face with my hands. "It's all going to be okay. Okay?"

She nods and takes a deep breath, leaning into my right palm. I grab her hand with my left and kiss the top.

"Okay," she says. "It's all going to be fine."

"Damn right." I settle back into my seat, keeping one arm around Kris's back on her chair. "Now, the cheese sticks here are a must. No choice there. Sadie will eat whatever. And I know you like supreme. So, how's that sound?"

She smiles and kisses my cheek.

"Sounds perfect."

Sadie strolls in about fifteen minutes later, carefree and happy, almost the exact second the food gets set down on the table.

"I am so sorry I am late!"

I roll my eyes, having known she would be.

She doesn't take her seat across from us but instead comes up behind Kris and hugs her around her shoulders. I wish I could have taken a picture of Kris's stunned face. I can't help but laugh as she pats Sadie's arm and looks to me for help.

"It's so nice to-"

"Sadie, let the woman get up, will you?"

"Oh! Gosh, I got so excited. I'm sorry!"

I shake my head and laugh while Kris scoots her chair out and stands up. She surprises me as she opens her arms and hugs Sadie in a more proper way.

"It's really nice to meet you. I've been so nervous so please excuse any gross sweat or stuttering."

I laugh again at Kris's admission and Sadie squeezes her a little extra before pulling back and gripping her arms.

"Don't be nervous about me. Please. I love you already and if you asked to meet Cameron tonight, I would have zero objection."

She is serious and I love her for it.

Kris looks down, almost embarrassed before hugging Sadie again and saying thank you.

Sadie winks at me over her shoulder before sitting down and digging into the pizza.

The meal goes like I thought it would. Sadie lightly questions Kris about her life, like any sane almost-thirty-year-old woman who is a little bit nosy.

"Where were you born?"

"Where did you go to college?"

"Did you grow up with pets?"

"What's your dads name?"

"Is he hot?"

She is certifiable.

"Alright, we're here to basically get your blessing Sadie. Kris isn't comfortable making plans to meet Cameron at some point without you being completely okay with the whole thing. So, tell her you're okay with it all. Please." I smile at my friend before I take a drink of my melting iced tea.

Sadie brushes her fingers off with a napkin and rolls her lips together.

"Well," she drawls.

I feel myself still. No way will she do the opposite of what I have been convinced she would do. There is no way.

She barks out a laugh and hits her knee. "I got you so good, Cars!"

"You," I say flatly and point at her, "are not funny."

"Yes, I am," Sadie says through a laugh, wiping at her eyes.

"Yes, she kind of is," Kris pipes in, smothering her own laugh behind her hand.

"Whose team are you on?" I demand, amusement in my voice.

"Yours, baby. Yours." Kris leans in and kisses me quickly on the cheek while still giggling.

I look to Sadie and find her smiling adoringly at us. My heart feels so fucking full.

"You're great Kris. Really. I trust Carter, and I trust you. Meet Cameron whenever. Let me know if you want help or whatever. Anything, name it. He'll adore you."

Kris and I smile at Sadie, and I nod my head.

"Now, if you'll excuse me. I have to get back to work and then get our kiddo. It was seriously so nice to meet you, Kris. I can just tell you and I will be fast friends." Sadie meets Kris at the front of the table, and they hug.

"Can I have Carter give me your phone number? Maybe we can get a pedicure or something before sandal weather is completely gone."

"I would love that! Yes. Cars, give your girl my number, yeah?"

I nod my head and stand to hug Sadie.

"I'll have Cameron call you tonight per the usual."

"Sounds good, Sades. Hey, thanks for everything."

Sadie leans in and whispers, "I love her."

I whisper back, "Me too."

"I know."

And with a wink directed at Kris, and a wave to us both, Sadie is out the door.

"She's great," Kris says while grabbing my hand. I step in front of her like she prefers and lead us to the door.

We get to her car far too quickly for my liking.

"What are you doing the rest of the day?" she asks as she leans her butt on her driver's door.

"Well, that's up to you I think," I say as I cage her in, placing my hands around her, on her car.

She plays with the strings hanging from the collar of my hoodie. "I have some work calls sporadically scheduled for the rest of the afternoon but nothing crazy. Do you want to come to the cabin and just hang out?"

I nuzzle into her neck and nod. "I'd love nothing more."

She runs her hands through my hair, lightly scratching at my scalp. It takes everything in me to not purr like a damn cat.

"Lead the way sweetheart."

Chapter Sixteen

I Love You This Big

Kris

I silently thank this morning me for having spruced up the living room and bathroom in a random bout of energy before leaving earlier.

"I've got a video call in like," I look at my watch, "fifteen minutes but it shouldn't take more than twenty minutes. And then I don't have anything until four."

"Whatever you've got to do, honey. I'm just glad to be here."

Carter leans in for a kiss as I close the front door. The kiss deepens. He holds my face with both hands, and I run mine through his hair. I don't know what is about these onyx locks of his but Lord have mercy, I never want to stop feeling them on my fingers.

We break apart and he finishes taking his boots off. I mentally note how nice it looks to have his worn, brown boots sitting next to my worn-in black Birkenstocks.

"There's some bottles of iced tea in the fridge and there's ice in the freezer if you need some." I point to the kitchen as I make my way to my makeshift office in the living room. "I use my AirPods so you can watch whatever and just hang out."

I feel weird all of a sudden, having him here just to sit while I work. Even if it is only a brief call.

Carter somehow reads me like he always does. "Seriously sweetheart, don't worry about me. I'm just happy to be here with you. Doing whatever for however long. It's fine."

He places a kiss on my forehead before sitting on the couch opposite me. I get my work stuff pulled up and we fall into an easy quiet.

Easy.

That is how it is with Carter. It's easy. And honestly, it makes me a little uncomfortable. How is it all this easy already? It's only been a couple of months, not even, and things are just... simple? He is simple. He is kind and good and generous, with his time and his effort. He is funny and smart, and I can't help but silently question when the other shoe will drop like it seems to do so often in my life.

I shake off my pessimistic thoughts and focus on the incoming video call.

When I quoted twenty minutes, I was apparently being very optimistic. Forty-five minutes later and this call is sucking the life out of me. I love my job, but my attention keeps flitting the incredibly patient and handsome man on the couch across from me.

He is the picture of relaxation. If I could paint, I would paint this— *him*. His hat is hanging on a jeans-clad knee that is bent as that ankle rests over his other knee. He has one arm draped and stretched over the back of the couch and the other is resting on his lap. His hair is perfectly mussed, not wild but not the combed look it is right after he showers. His white long sleeve shirt looks so bright against the brown fabric of the couch. It is honestly unfair how absolutely beautiful he is.

We make eye contact before I look back down at my coworker. Paul has nothing on Carter. Though, I doubt Paul would mind me thinking that. He would probably laugh and tell his husband of thirty years what a bonehead I am.

I laugh at myself, feeling a bit delirious after all the numbers and work-nonsense. It has nothing to do with Carter's blue eyes unintentionally stealing my attention.

I hear him move around but don't look up. I feel as though if I do, I won't be able to look away again and I can feel this conversation begin to wrap up.

I catch his white shirt flash out of the corner of my eye and decide to risk it. He is seemingly not paying me any attention. I hold in a laugh as I watch what he is doing. The elevator behind the couch bit, with the most serious face. I am talking full on *My Big Fat Greek Wedding* moment. After his descent down in his "elevator" he makes the ascent. From there, still not paying me any direct heed, he unrolls a newspaper that he must have gotten from the kitchen counter and begins to read it. He checks his watch, that he is not wearing by the way, before rolling the paper back up and shoving it under his arm, breathing air into his palm to check his breath, and then exiting the nonexistent box he is in.

I am dying. I have got tears coming out of my eyes from trying so hard not to laugh. My face is giving it all away and one quick peek at Paul tells me he is beyond confused and a little peeved. But I don't have it in me to stop the shenanigans.

"Paul, I am so sorry. But something's come up and I've got to run. Sounds like we've got," I choke on a laugh as Carter takes imaginary stairs downwards but pretends to stumble on the way, "everything under control. I'll chat with you tomorrow, yeah?"

We say goodbye and I let out a cackle like I have never made before. I am howling at the absolute hooligan that is now straight faced and standing with his thick arms crossed over his chest.

"Something funny, Miss Atwater?"

I rise, closing my laptop and wiping at my eyes. "Nothing at all, Mister Barker. Nothing funny at all."

I put my knees on the couch, setting my hands on the back and leaning forward towards Carter. He puts his hands next to mine and bends at the waist so that we are eye level.

"I'm sorry that was far longer than I had anticipated."

His smile turns wry as he waggles his eyebrows, and he chuckles. I roll my eyes and sit back on my heals.

"My next call isn't for an hour, and I know for a fact that one won't last more than a few minutes. My boss is quick with the mid-week check-ins."

Carter smiles and walks around the couch before sitting next to me and pulling me into his lap.

"I'm going to squish you."

He only pulls me closer to him, nuzzling my neck with his nose. His scruff rubs under my chin, and I wonder about whether or not that spot will be red for more than a few moments.

And then I wonder why I find myself hoping it will be.

"I've missed you these past couple of days," Carter says into my hair.

"I've missed you as well."

The nuzzling turns into kissing which turns into panting which turns into a quick moment of chaotic disrobing.

"Bedroom?" I breathe against Carter's mouth.

"No way. You look too perfect on this couch, all soft curves and porcelain skin. The perfect contrast to the dark, rough couch." His kisses trail down my neck and continue in their downward direction.

"It's so bright in here though," I whisper.

Fuck insecurities and all that goes along with them. This man makes me feel fine as hell and no one has ever asked me to put my clothes back on. But still... The afternoon sun is not forgiving, and I *did* eat pizza like two hours ago and now he's here, literally face deep in the "soft curves" and I am feeling a little panicky.

"Sweetheart, I'd turn the fucking sun up if I could in here."

Well, okay then.

After christening the couch of this cabin, feeling fully scandalized and absolutely relaxed, I check my reflection in the mirror.

No make-up. A faint, natural blush on the rounds of my cheeks. My freckles are extra vibrant from the days spent with Carter on his porch. My highlights have grown to a more golden bronze color that looks like intentional strands instead of just regrowth in my dark mass, and it is full of volume after having Carter's hands all up in there.

It's the light in my eyes though, that makes my smile grow. The little twinkle, the shimmer, the glisten, that I notice in the grassy green color of my irises. It was not there two months ago— that sparkle. I have not seen a shine like that in quite a long time. And it's not lost on me in the slightest, what a gift it is.

To look happy.

To *be* happy.

The rest of the afternoon goes by in a flash. My boss and I talked for three minutes and thirteen seconds. Carter ran to the store right before I called her to get some ingredients for supper.

He has cooked me the most incredible casserole tonight. He called it "Mexican Meatloaf" and said his great aunt Shirley found it on the back of a Minute Rice box decades ago. It was incredible and I sent the recipe to my mom. She promised to make it this week after she sends my dad to the store and then to report back.

Knowing her, she will call me before she has even finished the first bite.

"Cameron's calling, want to say hi?"

I choke on absolutely nothing. I don't know why I allow myself to get so nervous over that sweet child. It has nothing to do with Cameron, I know that much.

What if he hates me? What if I can't have kids because some higher power knows that I *should not* have kids? That I am just not biologically equipped for that? That I am predisposed to being hated by children and so me not being able to have any just saved me and the nonexistent children the trouble of a bad time?

"Sweetheart?" Carter's face is a mix of calm and concern. "If not, it's okay. No pressure."

"Yes!" I say too loudly.

He just laughs at me, and I bury my face in my hands. "Answer his call and give me thirty seconds to get it together."

"You've got it honey." Carter kisses my temple. "Bubba!"

"Daddy!"

Gosh his little voice is so damn sweet.

"How was daycare today pal? You work on your numbers again?"

"Yep!"

Cameron counts to twelve for his dad and Carter's smile grows with each number.

My shitty ovaries are screaming right now.

"Hey, pal. I want to show you my friend, Kris."

Carter pans the phone to where I am, next to him on the couch. I wave a very small wave and smile a genuine smile.

"Hey Cameron. That was some expert counting."

He just smiles and says thank you and waves back and suddenly I feel so stupid for being so scared that a two-year-old was going to immediately loathe me entirely.

Carter keeps the phone on the two of us, his arm around my shoulders now and my head leaning towards him. The conversation flows. As smoothly as one can with a toddler on the other end of the call. Carter tells Cameron to listen to his mom and have sweet dreams and that he will see him this weekend. Cameron tells us both goodnight and my heart flutters a bit at his sweet little goodbye—the fact that I was included in it.

"He's wonderful," I say as I rest my head on Carter's shoulder.

"Yeah, he is." He kisses the top of my head. "Can we maybe," he treads lightly, "discuss you meeting him?"

I sit up and turn so I'm facing him fully. It makes sense why he sounds nervous to ask me that. I am a spazz. And I have acted especially spazzy about his son. Regardless of the fact that it is not personal. It's me and absolutely *not* Cameron, I would feel uncomfortable too if I were Carter.

"I'm terrified that he's going to hate me and that a small part of why I can't have children is because I'm inherently predisposed to be hated by all kids."

It comes out very fast and very aggressively and I am left feeling very exposed and embarrassed because I know it sounds insanely stupid.

Carter turns his body towards me, his bent knee resting under mine.

"Sweetheart." His voice is full of sympathy and a little amusement.

"I know, it's insane. I am insane. But I just don't want him to not like me. I like to be liked, Carter. And if your son doesn't like me for whatever reason... He's his own little person. He has the right to choose who he's a fan of, and who he isn't. And I'm not above buying his affection. You tell me his favorite candy and I'll go to the dollar store in town right now and stock up." I take a breath and try to tame the spiral. "I want him to like me." My voice is quiet.

Carter reaches up and tucks a piece of my hair behind my ear and I look up, meeting his eyes. The sun kissed skin is crinkled in the corners, his smile wide.

"Cameron will like you, Kris. Cameron will *love* you. Just like I love you."

The sureness and lack of hitch shocks me in his admission.

"You love me?" I whisper.

Carter brushes the pad of his thumb over my cheek, then down the bridge of my nose. It settles on my chin, his grip light but firm.

"I love you, Kris Katherine Atwater. I think I've loved you for five years. Ever since I first saw you in your Johnny Cash t-shirt and those bright red lips. And I know I love you now with your brown sweatpants and nothing but the freckles on your face."

I take a breath. My eyes burn and my nose tingles. I play with the crease in my aforementioned brown sweatpants on my thigh, but I don't take my eyes off of his.

"I love you too, Carter Arlington Francis Barker. Wholly. Fully. Irrevocably. I love-"

His lips are on mine, and he pours that love into me. I pour mine right back into him. I love you's are whispered between the both of us, felt in every breath.

By the time we lay down to shut our eyes for the night I am left feeling utterly loved and coveted and cherished. More so than I have ever felt before.

Yet the feeling, the reminder of the other impending shoe that always finds its way to the floor of whatever room I am standing in, does not stray too far from my sleepy mind.

Chapter Seventeen

Watching You

Carter

My palms are sweaty and as that thought crosses my mind I want to briefly rap to some Eminem. I resist the urge and instead just wash my hands, unnecessarily, and dry them off. I don't know the actual reason I am freaking out. Well, I do. But it is *so* stupid.

They will love each other. There is no way they won't. Cameron and Kris are going to be best fucking friends.

But what if they aren't?

The little voice in my head needs to shut the hell up.

I hear tires crunching against rocks as someone pulls into the driveway. I have my front door open and the window to the screen door pulled up. The breeze from this unusually warm late September day is a welcome guest in my old house. The dirt it kicks up, I could do without. But for fresh air, I will dust.

I don't drop the bright yellow dishtowel I am starting to think might be more of a comfort-towel, as I walk to the door and watch Sadie get Cameron out of the back of her car. My chest aches with love and the anxiety takes a back seat.

"Bubs!" I shoot out the door and bound down the steps. Cameron meets me almost halfway and throws himself at me. It is like this every time, even if it has only been a day since we last saw each other. And I know someday that might change The jumping will stop and then the hugging will loosen and maybe lessen, and then someday he might even just shake my hand. So, for now I soak it in. Every time, I let it consume me— this love I have for my kid.

"Hey, Cars. How are you doing?" Sadie reaches us and hugs me with one arm while mussing up Cameron's dark brown hair.

Where mine is a nice black and Sadie's is a warm brown, Cameron is the happy medium between us. All pale skin, like his mom, freckles everywhere the sun touches. Green eyes from somewhere on Sadie's side, and a beautiful shade of brown hair that reminds me of hot chocolate.

"Good, Sades. You?" I hug her back and we watch as Cameron gets on his little red tricycle near the garage.

"Good, good. Going to Omaha with Lance once I get back to the house. He says hi." Her smile widens and her eyes become a little love-sick.

I bump my shoulder into hers. "Happy looks good on you, Sades."

"It doesn't look so bad on you either, Cars."

Sadie runs down Cameron, hugging and kissing the life out of the lucky kid.

"I'll see you Monday after daycare, bud. I love you." I hear her kiss him loudly one more time before she high-fives me on her way to her car. "Kris coming over, yeah?"

I move some random rocks around with my bare foot. "Yeah, she'll be here in about an hour."

"Lose the towel and relax, Carter. He'll love her," she yells from halfway into her car.

Some tension leaves my shoulders and I toss the towel over my shoulder.

"Have a good time. We'll call you tonight."

Once Sadie is gone and the literal dust settles, I lightly snap my towel at Cameron's little toddler butt before picking him up and throwing him over my shoulder.

"Dad!" His giggles fill my ears, my soul.

I set him down on the steps before kneeling in front of him. "I need to talk to you quick, okay bud?"

Cameron plays with a loose string on his gray hoodie and nods.

I know he isn't even three. I understand this. But he is a smart almost-three. And even if he wasn't, I prefer open communication regardless, so he would get it anyways.

"I've got a friend coming over in a bit to hang out with us."

"Unc Kenny?"

"No, not Uncle Kenny. But maybe he'll come hang out tomorrow with us." I move to sit next to Cam. He's moved on from the stray string to a rogue dandelion that he pulled out of his pocket. He must have found that while I was talking to his mom. "This friend is really extra important to me. Your mom knows her, they're friends. Her name is Kris and I really like her. So, she's going to come over and hang out. Maybe eat some supper with us. She might come over to play with us a lot from now on. Is that okay?"

I had low expectations for this conversation. He is a toddler. And this is a new thing. For both of us.

He doesn't look up at me as he asks, "she like dine-saurs?"

I laugh. I fucking love this kid.

"You know bud, I bet she loves dinosaurs. You'll have to show her yours when she gets here, yeah?"

"Yeah, 'kay."

Before I can even say another word, Cam is off and running through the yard, screeching awful sounding dinosaur noises and flapping his arms like a bird.

That is what we do for the next hour. I watch him act out his best prehistoric animals.

I hear her before I see her. The quiet of living in the country provides great surround sound.

Four tires, dark blue Toyota, tinted windows, a green rosary is hanging from the rearview mirror. Dark hair, down and curled today. Her usual black framed glasses. A smile that lights up my entire world.

I don't know I'm doing it until I am reaching for the handle of her door and a yellow towel gets in my way.

"Damnit," I mutter before throwing it onto my shoulder again.

"Hi baby," her voice exits her car before she does.

Kris pauses, looking around the car like she is forgetting something.

"Oh!" She snaps her fingers and reaches into the backseat.

As she gets out of the car, I do my usual ogling. Leggings, a loose white t-shirt that has Travis Kelce's face all over it in a bunch of colored squares, black sandals, and a light brown sweater.

She always looks so cozy and warm and sexy.

She leans up, both hands full, and kisses my cheek.

"Hi sweetheart," I get out while checking her hands. "What's with the present?" I move to grab her unnecessarily large water cup out of her other hand.

"I got Cameron a little 'hey I'm dating your dad and I want you to like me' gift." Her bare cheeks turn rosy, and she looks around. "Where-"

"Dating dad?"

She startles, her eyes going wide, and her empty hand goes to her chest. I laugh and Cameron comes out from behind my legs. I had felt him grab me almost the second I stopped at her door.

"Yeah, Cam. Dating dad."

Her eyes shoot to mine, and she looks like she doesn't know what to do. It is then that I realize I don't really know what to do either.

I look at her and then Cameron and even though I know now is not the time, I nearly drop to my knees and thank God for this moment. For these two people. For this very second of time where my son is holding onto my legs and my girl is holding onto my arm.

I get down on a knee and look up at Kris. Her blinking increases and I laugh before pulling her hand to get her down here with me. Once she is eye level with Cameron and I, I tell him, "This is the friend I was telling you about. Cameron, this is Kris. Kris," I look at her and wink, "this is my kid. Cameron Carter Barker."

She is quiet for a moment, and Cam can be shy so he's matching Kris. I open my mouth to say that we should go inside when she leans in, squeezing my hand.

"Cameron Carter Barker. Do you know that you are incredibly beautiful?"

"That me?"

We both look at where he is pointing before laughing together.

"Yes, yeah, it is. I got you a present. A thank you for letting me come hang out with you and your dad."

Cam jumps on the opportunity to open a gift.

"Dine-saurs!" He is jumping up and down, holding two new dinosaur toys and smiling like it's Christmas.

Kris and I stand up after he runs into the house, zero fucks given about us now. I look over at her and catch her already looking at me. Her beautiful smile meeting her incredible eyes.

"You did good, sweetheart," I say into her hair as I press my lips to her temple. "Really good, baby."

She turns her body into mine and hugs me tightly.

"Let's go in. I'll get supper started and you can tell me about the rest of your week."

I throw my arm around her shoulders, and we start walking. Her arm slips around my waist and grabs at my black t-shirt.

"Carter, I just saw you the day before yesterday. You act like it was Monday since I saw you." Her laugh is melodic and light and my anxiety over this whole thing is nonexistent now.

"It felt like years," I say honestly.

I know I have it bad. I have known that from the moment I saw her in that stadium in South Dakota. I have tried to keep that on lockdown, be low key. I am giving up that façade though. I simply can't do it. It feels like a lie— acting as though I don't feel as much as I do.

"Hey," I say just before the door.

Kris looks up at me and smiles.

Like she can read my mind she beats me to what I was going to say.

"I love you. Thank you for inviting me over to meet Cameron."

"Anytime. Literally. At all. Ever." I kiss her softly. "I love you."

Chapter Eighteen

Honey, Honey

Kris

If I were not already in love with Carter, seeing him as a dad would have sealed that deal. Sweet Lord, my ovaries. He is incredible. And it does not at all feel like any of it is being put on as some sort of show.

The way he is gentle but firm with his rules. The way he musses Cameron's hair like he can't help but feel him— physically love on him, every time he walks anywhere near him. The way Cameron smiles every single time because he loves his dad with every fiber of his being. It is all so sweet, my teeth almost hurt.

Right now, Cameron is being put to bed. Carter is in his bedroom, per their usual bedtime routine that I have heard all about. The tucking in, the kisses, the reading, the little talks. I am sitting on Carter's couch, my feet out in front of me on the cushions with my ankles crossed. Cameron handed me one of his new dinosaurs before running off to his bedroom and I haven't set it down. I've just been sitting here, content. I move its little plastic legs and poke at its tiny fake teeth. My brain is not running a million miles a minute, but it also isn't quiet right now. I'm not thinking about the potential impending shoe and I am not feeling sad about missing home. Quite the opposite really.

"Dime for what's going on in that mind?"

I don't jump at his voice. My body is too calm for that, I think.

"I loved tonight."

Carter comes around the couch. He changed into some black sweatpants between the last time I saw him and now. They do some real funny things to me, those sweatpants.

"Eyes are up here, sweetheart."

I hear his smirk before I see it, so I roll my eyes. He brings my feet into his lap, rubbing them one at a time. I let my head fall back against the arm of the couch and hold the dinosaur to my chest.

After a few moments of quiet companionship, I ask quietly, "Did he like me?"

Carter laughs a quiet laugh and runs his hand up my calf, working the muscles there. Normally having someone touching me so intimately somewhere I feel insecure about would be off-putting. That is not at all the case here though.

"You see that dinosaur he gave you?" He looks at the one I haven't put down and I nod. "Cameron is territorial. He shares, but usually it's with some coercion. I didn't ask him to do that. He was halfway to his room when he stopped, turned around, and walked back to give that to you. That was all on his own. You're a ten, baby. Five stars."

I smile and clutch the little toy harder to me before setting it down on the table in front of us with the utmost care. I climb to my knees and put myself in Carter's lap, my knees on either side of his thighs. Running my hands through his hair and rubbing his scalp I press kisses to his brow, his cheeks, his nose, his chin. The stubble there scratches at my lips, and I take a moment to run my mouth over the scruff there a few more times.

I pull back, my gaze landing on his, before saying, "Thank you for this. For letting me into this part of your life. I don't take that for granted." I kiss his lips softly. "I don't take you for granted. I don't take the fact that you let me meet that sweet, wonderful, smart little boy for granted." My kisses move lower, running over his jaw and down his neck. His hands grip my hips, his thumbs running over the creases there. "Just," I bring my eyes back to his, "thank you. I love you. I loved meeting Cameron. I loved watching you be all Hot Farm Daddy."

Carter laughs, almost too loudly for post-bedtime, before asking, "Hot-farm-daddy, huh?" His smirk turns mischievous, and his eyes track down my face, down my neck, over my chest. They map out my entire being.

"Sherry came up with it," I laugh. "But It's true," I say as I lean in and kiss the top of his head. I pull back again. "I should probably get going, though. I'm sure he'll be up early for you."

His grip tightens and his eyes shoot to mine. "Whoa, you're not staying the night?"

His genuine disappointment makes my heart stutter. "I didn't want to assume or put you in a weird spot. Responsible adults and all that."

"Sweetheart. First, from now on, always assume you're staying the night. Second, I don't mean this in a disrespectful adult way, but I think we've got some leeway here with the whole 'Cam is only two' thing." He nuzzles his nose into my neck. "Like, I think if he were five or eight or twelve, shit would need to be clear and concise as far as things like sleepovers go. But he doesn't even know what that is in the most basic way. I think he'll just see it as the new norm, if that makes sense. Like, he'll just see me and his normal Saturday morning waffles and then you and it'll be next to nothing to him as long as the syrup is poured the second he sits down."

I laugh and rest my chin on the top of his head. My hands are still rubbing at his scalp and his are roaming literally everywhere they can reach.

It does make sense. I don't know much about kids, but I think that Carter knows what is best for Cameron. And I do not feel anywhere near uncomfortable or nervous like I did just a few days ago.

"Saturday morning waffles, you say?"

"Homemade," he whispers against my neck. "Buttermilk," he moves lower. "Betty Crocker Original syrup," and lower still, each phrase punctuated by a kiss.

"I love you," I giggle as his almost-beard tickles at my skin.

Carter groans into the spot on my chest he is paused at. "Say it again. And again. And again."

So, I do. I say it while we walk, or more like shuffle, to his bedroom. I say it while we continue those sweet, delicate, reverent kisses in the dark. And I say it the next morning, matching messy hair and morning breath, him in his blue briefs and me in a pair of his basketball shorts and my t-shirt.

And I can't help but to tell that other shoe to fuck off and hope that I get to say "I love you" to this handsome man for a really long time. Indefinitely, really.

Chapter Nineteen

Baby Shark

Carter

Saturday mornings are typically my favorite mornings when Cameron is here. Today is not an exception to that rule. This morning I woke up with my girl in my arms, and in my clothes. I always make waffles for Cameron and I. He always makes an absolute mess with the syrup so then we do a bath and spend the rest of the day putzing around on the farm or running to town for groceries. It's always a day of some rest and getting things ready for the week. Usually, it is just the two of us. But Kris is here now. And I don't think I am the only one happy about that.

"She's a hit, Ken."

"Of course, she is. And it's not like Cam is hard to impress. Not that Kris isn't great."

I huff a laugh. "She's incredible and Cameron is incredible and together, man. I don't think I have ever felt such genuine happiness, Ken. Both of them here, under the same roof— *my* roof. It's like a dream I didn't even know I had."

"You sound like a sap, my guy. I love it for you."

"Cameron wants you to come over for supper tonight."

"His wish is my command. See you three later."

Three.

I walk back inside after having moved Kris's car from behind where I parked the pickup in the garage.

"Alright you two-" I stop halfway to the couch where I last saw Kris and Cam.

When I had walked outside, not five minutes ago, Cam had been sitting on the floor with his dinosaurs and Kris had been sitting on the couch with her laptop doing some small things for work. Now... Lord have mercy. If my heart could explode and I would survive it, this would do it.

Kris is still on the couch, looking cute as hell. The little jokester had packed an overnight bag just in case and still made me panic thinking she was leaving last night. She has on a pair of light denim jeans that hit just above her ankle and hang loose on her smooth legs with a couple holes in the knees that make me want to reach my hand up there and run them all over the smooth, pale skin hidden there. Her shirt is another loose black t-shirt, and her hair is pulled back into her pink clip.

I love on Cam a lot. I am always messing with his hair or holding his hand or rubbing his back. And the same goes for Kris. I want to pull the clip out and run my fingers through her dark strands, pick out the lighter pieces that are scattered throughout, one by one.

And then there is Cameron. In his little blue jeans and a bright blue long-sleeve shirt. He's propped up on Kris's lap, one hand resting on his little belly and the other holding her hand on his small lap. Her other hand is holding one of his books. From here I can see it, *The Little Blue Truck*. His head is leaning fully on her chest, tucked into her neck and her chin is resting on his thick hair. She's reading to him in a bunch of terribly perfect voices to match the characters.

"HONK HONK! I'm coming through, I've big important things to do," she half-yells, doing her best dump truck imitation.

I choke on a laugh, and she looks over Cam's head at me, smiling widely. My heart, I swear to all, stops and then starts on that smile.

I walk over to them, pressing a kiss to the top of each of their heads.

"Ready when you two are," I say. The words sound so foreign and new but so right and welcome.

I lean against the back of the couch, watching Cameron snuggle into Kris and listening to Kris read to Cameron. Kris and Cameron... My entire world, right here on this couch. I bring a hand the back of my neck and take a deep breath, fighting the tingling in my nose.

After a beautiful reading and some laughs about how much Kris can't sound like a toad, we get settled in the car. Cameron kicks his little booted feet around while he sits in his big car seat and watches a movie on the back of my headrest.

"Is there a Starbucks in town?"

"Well, there isn't one in Holdrege. But we can get groceries in Kearney. They've got a few."

"Oh, no, it's totally okay! I don't need one, I was just curious."

I grab her hand from where it was pressed under her thigh and bring it to my lips. I press a kiss to each knuckle and run my thumb over her freckles on her wrist.

"Kearney is fine, sweetheart. More options for lunch afterwards anyways."

Kris smiles and bites the inside of her bottom lip. "Well, if you're sure."

"I'm sure about a lot of things, honey." I wink at her, and her cheeks turn pink. "I'm sure that Cameron will get a better nap this way on the way home. I'm sure that Hy-Vee will be far too busy for my liking, but they have the best produce. I'm sure that Ken is going to test my patience with each compliment he throws your way tonight. And I'm sure that getting the woman I love the Starbucks she wants is the least that I can do today."

"I love you too," is all she says while she sets our hands on the center console between us. "Oh!" she starts. "Is there a Target?"

I laugh and tell her yes. I have never been excited to go to that store until now.

Cameron decided that Target would be the best place to try out some independence. And also, a good time to try and successfully steal my woman. And I have never felt better about watching my girl hold another guy's hand.

We ordered some drinks; a hot brown sugar espresso for me, an iced vanilla latte for Kris, and a small chocolate milk on ice for Cam. Kris said it will make him feel like he is a grown up drinking coffee like his dad.

It did. I had never seen him so excited over a beverage.

Then Cam chose to not ride in the cart, which is new. He *then* decided to walk ahead of me and drag Kris along with him. Her coffee in her other hand and his not-coffee curled into his chest. Kris's dark blue nails are such a contrast on both of their light hands.

It is fucking adorable.

I do my job, pushing the cart and sipping on my drink, minding my own business. Kris stops every now and then to pick up a coffee mug or a kitchen towel and I smile to myself, making mental notes of what she smiles at most. She puts it all back, every time. We get to the back of the store where they have seasonal stuff up. Right now it's Halloween costumes and candy and decorations. Cameron squeals with excitement before dragging Kris with him to the costumes.

"Dine-saur!"

I round the corner and see him pointing at what is actually a shark costume. But he's two, so I don't correct him.

"You want to be a dinosaur for Halloween bud?"

"Yes!" He jumps up and down, his little shirt raising a little bit and showing off his round tummy.

Kris starts looking for his size and puts it in the cart when she finds it.

"You dine-saur too, Kiss," Cameron tells her while he pulls her around the isles.

"Gosh, I don't know if they have one that'll fit me bud. But we can definitely look."

Luck is on our side today because there sure is a shark costume that will fit perfectly on Kris. Cameron whoops and hollers and cheers and I join in while Kris smiles and blushes.

"There isn't one for your dad though, Cam."

"S'okay," he says with a shrug.

"I'm chopped liver now, sweetheart." I kiss her forehead and tell Cameron it's time to go. "And more than happy to be."

Kris links her arm with mine after I put Cameron in the back of the cart and the three of us head upfront to pay for their new Halloween costumes. I send a picture to Sadie and laugh when she replies.

> *Thank God he's found someone else to wear that shit.*

I show Kris and laugh as she asks, "She's not upset right?"

"Absolutely not. She doesn't mind dressing up with Cam for Halloween, obviously. But she definitely won't mind not doing it either." I laugh again and Kris smiles. "He loves you, you know? Cam. He's a big fan."

"I think I might be a bigger fan of him, Carter." She leans in and presses a kiss to my cheek before taking the cart and Cameron towards the door. She pauses and waits for me to catch up.

And I do. I follow after them like it is the most natural thing in the world.

Chapter Twenty

Time Warp

Kris

Halloween is one of my most favorite holidays. The spooky movies, the foggy mornings, the cold weather. Candy and goblins and hot chocolate with a little more than a splash of Bailey's.

I have always loved to be the one to hand out the candy, see all the cute kids in their costumes and wave to the parents as they stood back and told their kids to say thank you. I would have *Hocus Pocus* on in the background. Before I knew I could not have kids, I would daydream about when I would be on the other side of trick or treating. After, I grew content with the idea of never being on that side.

Tonight though, I am a part of the trick or treating and telling someone to say thank you and holding a bag when it starts to drag on the sidewalk. I get to hold my little buddy's hand and smile as doors open and bowls of candy get joyfully hoisted into view.

As a shark.

Well, as a shark that is trying to be a "dine-saur".

Cameron and I have matching shark suits. They are a super pale, almost gray blue color. One piece, cinched at the ankle and a hood on top that has a row of teeth sitting just above our eyes. We each have a dorsal fin on top of our heads. We look cute as heck.

Carter has not stopped smiling since Cameron and I did a runway walk for him and Sadie and Lance at the house before heading into town. It's getting dark as we finish up, now headed back to Carter's pickup. Sadie and Lance are going to Omaha for the rest of the week as a little anniversary getaway, so Cameron is headed to Carter's and will stay there for the next week.

I don't know who is more excited; me, Cam, or Carter.

Sadie gives Cameron a bunch of cute kisses all over his little face before telling him she loves him and that she will call him every night. She hugs me and Carter and not a single second of it feels forced or awkward.

If you had told me three months ago that my newest friend would be the mother that shares a child with the man I'm in love with, I would have laughed at you. For every part of that statement.

But here I am, hugging Carter's baby mama, my new friend, and getting ready to go spend the week with my boys.

My boys.

I do not know when it became that, when they became *mine. Both* of them. But they did and they are, and I have never been more grateful for anyone in my life. It has been about a month since I met Cameron and we quickly became best friends. He's incredible. He is smart and funny and a little mouthy which has to come from Sadie because Carter never knows how to deal with his little quips. Cameron is beautiful and kind and I love him.

I do. I love Cameron with a piece of my heart that I did not even know functioned.

I look at him sometimes, just to watch him, and I am in awe. Because how can I love someone that is not mine? How can it be possible to feel so protective and charmed and blessed to just know him when I didn't grow him, and I have not been here from the beginning? Yet, I am all of those things with Cameron.

The word "stepmom" feels premature but if this is what it feels like to be one, to love as one— God bless stepparents and their hearts.

I watch the way his eyes light up every time a plate of food gets put in front of him, the little foodie. The way he giggles loudest when he gets tickled right in the middle of his tiny shoulders. He is freckled, *everywhere*. But he has got the cutest, roundest, most perfect little freckle on the very top of his right ear. He can count to thirteen now, and when he sings the ABC's and gets to the LMNOP part, it is like a symphony to my ears. It is perfection even though it really is not at all.

I don't know how it feels to be a mom, not in the most biological way. But I do know this; I love Cameron Carter Barker like he is my family.

As we all get ready for bed, Carter getting Cameron out of his costume and into his orange and black striped jammies that he and I picked out last week at Target, I slip on my own dark green sweats and one of Carter's faded t-shirts, this one is orange. I sit on the edge of Carter's bed, waiting for him to come in when I hear him call for me from Cam's room.

I don't run, but I also don't take my time getting to his room.

Carter kisses me on the cheek as he leaves and says with a smile, "Kid wants you to read to him tonight." And then he is gone. Down the hall and out of sight.

I look from the hall to where Cameron is laying down. His little bed and his little room with little *everythings*. Things that I had not thought I would get to see or experience for the last few years. I do not take them for granted. The dinosaur night light. The random splotch of stickers, some half peeled, near the floor on the light blue wall. His twin sized bed that looks like a king when his small body is snuggled in the middle of it. I watch him scoot towards the wall and smile at me, his sleepy green eyes sucking me into his world.

"What are we reading tonight?" I ask as I settle onto his bed next to him.

He scoots into me, resting his head on the arm behind him and turning his body to face mine a little bit.

"Nuggle bug," he whispers. His voice is groggy, and his eyes are half closed.

I pick up *You're My Little Cuddle Bug* off of the table next to his bed. I know this is what gets read to him every night here.

I finish reading to Cameron and go to slide my arm out from under him. He opens his eyes and watches me stand. I brush his hair back a little bit and give him a kiss on his forehead.

"Sweet dreams, buddy," I whisper into his hair.

"Luh you, Kissy."

I freeze, entirely unprepared to have his sweet voice come out with those words. My eyes sting and the bridge of my nose tingles as I kiss him softly one more time and whisper, "I love you too, Camy."

I stand up and pull his navy comforter up to his chin and look down at him before turning towards the door. I almost yelp when I see Carter standing there. His grey sweatpants doing their job—damn well I might add. He has no shirt on and while usually that is where my focus might stretch for an unforeseen amount of time... Right now, it is his eyes. The bright blue is almost magnified behind the small lines of tears welling there on his bottom lashes.

I walk into his open arms and tuck my head into the crook of his neck. He rests his cheek on the top and I hear him sniffle.

"You big softy," I joke.

I love that he has emotions.

"I love you," he says back.

"I love you too." I look up and kiss his jaw.

"Move in with us." He whispers it but he does not shy away from it.

Without hesitation, not missing a beat, I say, "Okay."

Chapter Twenty-One

Home

Kris

Moving in with Carter and Cameron was as easy as everything else has been with them so far. Kris three months ago, right before driving her sad ass down here, would be incredibly concerned about when the simplicity would end. Kris today is just taking it one day at a time and enjoying the insane, but beautiful ride.

The owner of the cabin did not mind at all and even offered to give back the money I had put down for the first half of November. I felt so bad about the last-minute cancellation that I did not accept his generous offer. But it was kind, nonetheless. My brother offered to ship down my things but then Carter asked if we could just go to North Dakota for Thanksgiving.

So that is what we are doing. We have an hour left of the drive and I do not think people understand the test a road trip with a new partner can be sometimes.

We passed ours with flying colors. Carter wanted to bring his pickup so we could haul more back. I informed him that I do not have much to bring back with me. Clothes and some books that will all fit in my car. So here he sits, driving my little Camry up the highway, drumming his fingers on the dash in front of the steering wheel where his wrist is resting. I watch him. All the time. Like a creep. But he does not mind, and I don't find it to be an embarrassing situation when he catches me checking him out.

I'm nervous as we get closer to Fargo. He is going to meet my family. And while I love my family— *adore them...* they can be a lot. They are nosy and loud and a bit rambunctious, and even for me sometimes they are too much.

Carter does not have a care in the world about it though. He seems genuinely excited to meet them and have them meet him. They will love him, of that, I am sure. I just hope he likes them too. I don't complain too much about them to Carter because I know how fortunate I am to have family in the first place. But I do feel the need to warn him of their... filter-less-ness.

"My mom will be all over you. Not in a creepy way," I amend, "but in a," I pause to think of how to say it. "She's going to hug you. A lot. And probably touch your face. She is very touchy. And she's going to ask personal questions and they're going to be asked in front of everyone because we are all nosy and she's the instigator. She's going to pry into us, and into you and Cameron, and she's going to beg to FaceTime him because I haven't let her yet. But you don't need to worry because I will tell her no right away because that's a lot for that sweet boy." I take a breath. "And my dad will try to get you to drink and eat anything and everything. And it's a lot of things. Lots of random beer that he's picked up over the last few grocery store runs. Lots of weird trail mixes and chips and flavored pretzels. I don't even know where he finds them all, but he does, and he will force them down your throat. You tell him no, Carter. If you don't want it, you just say the word and I'll have your back. No pressure with them. My brother will probably look mean but he's harmless. Like a gnat. He's a know-it-all and kind of bossy and tries to play patriarch because my dad is a fucking lunatic sometimes. Not in the crazy, watch out for your hair in the middle of night getting buzzed off kind of way but he's just a bit wild. But Bryce will try to pry about shit that my mom will forget about and then Sherry," I breathe in and sigh. "Sherry is great. She's funny and smart and sweet and don't tell Sadie but Sherry's my best friend. Probably neck and neck with Sadie now honestly. But don't tell Sherry that!"

I look over, putting down my hands that were just flying through the air like they were trying to land airplanes. Carter has one fist at his mouth, the other hand resting on the steering wheel, and his cheeks are beat red from holding in his laughter.

I cross my arms over my chest. "Well, go on then. Let it out, killer."

I roll my eyes as he busts a gut at my expense. Which is fair and totally relaxes me. He will do just fine with my family. I know this.

It is *me* I am worried about, I think. My family sees me one way— the way I was just a few months ago. A shell of myself. An anxious mess of trauma and depression, even if I was healing myself slowly. And now...

Now I am blissfully happy and living a life I only ever dreamed of years ago. I think I am just nervous that they will treat me like the broken person I was and not recognize the growth and hard work that I have done with myself since I left, and even before then. The bad will outweigh the good to them and then they might try to enlighten Carter about how much of a mess I was and then he will see me like that.

I shake my head, clearing it of those thoughts.

"It'll all be fine, sweetheart," Carter says as he takes my hand, bringing it to his lips. "Perfectly fine."

I nod my head and hum in agreement as he turns the corner to my parents' house.

"It'll be fine."

"Dime for what's going on in that mind, honey?"

I turn to look at Carter. I love when he says that.

"I just want you to love me still by the time we leave." I feel so small as I say the words aloud.

"Oh baby." His voice is all sympathy. "Kris, you have to know that I will love you when we leave and every day after, right?"

I nod, chewing on the inside of my lip. Carter parks in the driveway and I move to get out. He doesn't let go of my hand though, so I turn to him, raising my brows.

"Give it to me, sweetheart— the worry. I want it. Let me hear it, please."

I nod and take a deep breath.

"Okay. I love you, right? Like whole heartedly, fully, deeply love you. I want to love you for the rest of my life. And it's not just you. It's Cameron too. I love him, Carter. Like I have never loved another person before. I love him in a way I didn't ever expect to be able to love someone after all that I have lost. So, here I am. In love with both you, and Camy, and it is bliss. It's easy and happiness and contentment and light and peace and it's all of the things that I thought I didn't deserve just mere months ago, Carter. So... I *am* worried. I'm worried that my family won't see how repaired I am. They won't see the non-damaged version of me now. And then what if I stop seeing that version of me? Or worse, you stop seeing that version of me? This version of me." I gesture to myself. "What if you start to see the broken girl? The woman with a body that's too big in the general public's opinion, a broken uterus, a sad but medicated brain, and a lot of damage that right now is just distant memories of a time past?" I take a breath and hold his hand tighter. "I love you. And I have never felt like this before, not even when I was married, Carter. So, I know what is at stake here. What's at stake every day. I don't take any of this— *us* for granted. And I don't normally stress about it, right? It's not like I sit here day in and day out terrified that I'm going to wreck this. But moments like now— the thoughts creep in and the panic takes over and I'm left to wonder if," I swallow, looking ahead at the license plate of Bryce's silver Ford Focus in front of us. "If this ends it will destroy me. If something goes wrong with us, then I won't be able to fix it. *Fix me.* I'll find myself on my shitty sectional that's in a storage unit right now, in a shitty apartment, *alone.* I'll wake up one morning to a copious number of take-out containers that desperately need thrown away, and a dry as fuck mouth because I haven't had a single *sip* of water in a week. I will be on that couch, by myself. In a world where I haven't showered in three days, I've lost fifteen pounds in a week, I haven't talked to my mom outside of two-word text messages in just as long." I look to my left and Carter's eyes lock on mine. He gives nothing away. "I don't want any of that. I don't want to be the broken girl again, even though it would be worse the next time. I don't want to be sick over you and Cameron and thinking to myself 'whoever he finds next will be lucky. She'll know him like I did but won't fuck it up like I did.' I don't want that for me or for you or for Cameron. And I know it sounds insane, that *I* sound insane, thus probably making my worries even more evident to you. But you asked so I'm telling you. Got your dimes worth."

I don't look back at him. His thumb sweeps soothing lines over the top of my hand, never having stopped, and I focus on the "My Wife's a Hot Teacher" sticker on Bryce's back window.

"Kris."

I do not move.

"Kris," his voice is soft and kind just like his heart.

"I hate that I hauled you all the way up here just to show you how insane I am."

"Sweetheart, please."

It's the please that gets me to look back at him. I know my parents are standing by the window at the front of their house, snooping. Watching whatever this is. But neither of us seems to care.

"There's a lot to unpack there. Some things are more important than others, but I would like it noted that your body, every ounce and centimeter of you, has me fucking *on*. All the time. Sweats, leggings, jeans, nothing. A bra, one of my shirts," he rolls his eyes. "I love it when you wear my shirts. But that's besides the point. Your body, your brain as it is, your uterus that is none of my business," he laughs, and I do too. "You, sweetheart, are everything to me. I didn't let myself ever dream of a life that was good, that was filled with constant love and affection. Not until Cam. And then it stopped there, with him. I never thought I would be lucky enough to have you show up even though I constantly wished for it. And now... *You are here*. With *me*. With *Cameron*. And the way you love us, Kris, the *both* of us," he breathes deeply. "It's fucking inspiring. It's earth shattering and knee weakening. It's more than I ever imagined for myself, and I would be a damn fool to ever look at you as anything other than an incredible blessing and the love of my life. Am I a fool, sweetheart?"

"No, Carter. You're not a fool."

"That's right, baby. I love you. Your worries aren't insane, but they also won't come to fruition. I hate that your brain tells you all that bull shit, but I am here to tell you that that's what it is— bull shit." He leans forward, his head over the center console, gripping the back of my neck and pulling me to him. "I love you. You love me. It's all alright, Kris. Okay?"

I nod, our foreheads meeting.

"I need to hear you say it, Kris. Please. So I know that you know that this is real and that I'm not going anywhere that you aren't."

"Yes, I hear you. I love you."

"I love you. Now," he pulls back, kissing me on the nose, "Let's go see what kind of pretzels your dad found because I haven't stopped thinking about those since you mentioned the possibility of them."

I laugh and shake my head. "You have no idea what you're in for, Carter."

Chapter Twenty-Two

My Girl

Carter

Kris wasn't exaggerating about any of it. The pretzels, all seven flavors. The amount of random beer John has stocked. The questions from Penny and Bryce. The sympathetic looks from Sherry because she has been where I am, stood where I'm standing. And the way they kind of tiptoe around my girl, like Kris is damaged or broken or something. The majority, I am good with. I love pretzels and beer and I definitely do not mind answering a million questions about my life.

Open book.

But the looks, the whispers to each other, and the pity in their eyes towards their daughter and sister. That shit is getting on my damn nerves. They mean well, I'm sure. I just don't get it, though. Kris has overcome some major trauma in recent years. She has done it all, basically alone, even when she was married. She is the strongest woman I have ever met, and her family treats her like she might break if they laugh too hard at something she says. Or if they don't laugh quite enough. As if she needs cushioning around every corner or comment. And maybe that was the case the last time they saw her, but that is not the case now.

She is a fucking superhero, this girl. And I can't believe they cannot see that.

"Hey you. Dime for what's on your mind?" Kris runs her hand from shoulder blade to shoulder blade and then down my arm to where my hand sits, on the arm of the Adirondack chair in John and Penny's backyard.

I take her hand in mine and take a drink of my beer. Some local vanilla brew that tastes good.

"I wish your family could treat you like the normal, strong, independent woman you are."

I feel her tense up, but she stays quiet.

"I just don't get it, Kris. They have to be able to see it." I look to her and she looks away. "You're brilliant and brave and they don't get it? It just makes me sad is all. Nothing against them, sweetheart. Not really."

"I know what you're talking about. I can only hope they start to see how well I'm doing at some point, and we go from there. That's all I can really do about it, Car."

"And that's plenty good enough." I bring her hand to my mouth, pressing my lips to each knuckle and spinning her little silver band around like I always do.

"Cam is going to call in the next few minutes," I say to her after a moment of quiet.

"I know, that's why I came out here."

I feign hurt, clutching my heart and say, "Ouch, you're not out here for me?"

We both laugh. Cameron does call the following minute and we talk to him for a good chunk of time. He tells us all about the parade he went to and the food they ate and how Lance carried him on his shoulders almost all day. He went a million miles a minute, but it was so good to hear his voice and see his face. I miss him when he isn't with me.

"I miss him."

I look at Kris, her chair closer to mine now than it was before the call.

"Me too," I say, leaning in and kissing the side of her head.

"Don't suppose you'd let us go home early?" she asks sweetly, batting her long lashes.

"No, baby. We've got plans, remember? You're taking me around town tomorrow. Showing me off," I pull her out of her chair and move her to my lap. "You mentioned a bookstore and showing me all your old stomping grounds."

She giggles. "I don't believe I used the phrase stomping grounds. But yes, we can do all of that tomorrow."

"And then, if by tomorrow night you want to leave a day early, I won't stop us."

Kris sits up and smiles widely. "Really?"

I press my forehead to her chest and laugh. "You kill me. Yes, really."

"Okay, bookstore and stomping shit tomorrow. It'll be wild because it's the day after Thanksgiving but it's fine. Then home Saturday. Maybe Sadie will let us grab Cam on our way home."

"I can sure ask her, dear."

We sit like this for a while. Kris in my lap, her head in between my shoulder and neck. I have one arm holding my beer that she is now sharing with me on her lap and the other is playing with the hair I have freed from today's pink clip.

"I love how much you love Cameron."

My comment jolts her a bit, it was really quiet.

"I love him like he's mine," she whispers.

"I know, sweetheart. I know."

"Mom, we'll be back by supper but please chill out. It's a short trip, I know. But we've got shit to do before the new week starts and cows to feed and Ken can't do it all by himself for like, more than three days. So, relax. Cameron misses his dad. We're going home tomorrow. It's fine. I call you almost every day. It's not as though we never speak."

I hear the North Dakotan accent hitting extra hard with every word Kris gets out. Her mom was unimpressed last night when Kris mentioned us going home a day early as we headed to bed. We had stayed up and played Tapple with John, Penny, Bryce, and Sherry. Bryce and Sherry left around eleven. When it was just the four of us it was still nice. No bickering or fighting, and Kris seemed like her normal self. Her mom every now and then would make some comment like "have you lost some weight, honey?" or "you've got some bags under your eyes, dear. Sleeping alright?" And I'm sure that's their normal but not having had to deal with parental situations, and not being a fan of the way this family talks to Kris sometimes, it grated on my nerves. I didn't mention it, but I did make sure to show Kris just how perfect and beautiful she is when it was just us last night before we went to sleep.

I go to round the corner but hear Kris clear her throat. Then I feel a hand lightly on my shoulder and turn to see John behind me with a finger to his mouth and shaking his head. He's the head of the house, and I am not yet comfortable enough to argue with the King of Flavored Pretzels. So, I listen.

"Mom, here's the thing. I think you think that I am broken still."

"Now Kris-"

"No." I smile with pride at my girl. "Listen please."

"Okay, honey. I'm listening."

Kris takes a deep breath and if I didn't think she was courageous before...

"I'm not damaged. I'm not broken. I'm not sad. I'm not some walking shell of who I used to be before Michael and the babies. I'm good, mom. I'm healthy for all intents and purposes. I am in love and loved. There's a little boy in Nebraska that calls me 'Kissy' and melts my heart every time he tells me he loves me. My job is still good. Michael did not ruin me. My uterus being a bitch did not ruin me. The miscarriages I had sucked, I know. I lived it. But that's just it mom. I *lived* it. I lived through it all and I'm doing so well and feeling so good. I don't know if I've lost weight because it's not something I give a shit about. The bags under my eyes have always been there because I'm pale and don't sleep like, that much almost ever. Especially now that I have a hot boyfriend who thinks I'm a babe."

John chokes on a laugh as we stand shoulder to shoulder in the hallway.

He whispers, "I knew Nebraska would be good for her. I just didn't know how good you would be *to* her. You and your son, you're welcome here any time, son." And with that he claps me on the shoulder before stepping towards the women of the house.

I am momentarily stunned. I've been called "son" before. Old guys during coffee hour at the fire hall, Ken's family sometimes. But the way he said it— the way his eyes kind of glossed over for a moment... It felt different this time. I take a steadying breath and shake myself out of those emotions. I will accept that offer, that token of acceptance.

"Well honey," John says as he stalks up to Kris and pulls her in for a hug. "I'm proud of you. I love you. I'm glad you're so happy." He kisses the top of her head before heading to the coffee pot.

Penny gets up off the stool she was occupying and does the same, genuinely and a little bleary eyed.

I sidle up to Kris and wrap her in my arms, kissing the top of her head.

"I'm proud of you," I say into her hair.

"I'm proud of me too," she says back on a giggle. "Ready to go see the town?"

"Where you lead, I'll follow, sweetheart."

Chapter Twenty-Three

I Can Do Better Than That

Carter

Fargo, North Dakota is as advertised. Cold, cheery, busy. We just walked into the bookstore that Kris has on our list of where we are going today. It smells like vanilla and paper, which feels very on brand for anything where Kris is concerned.

"I won't be long, just want to have a look," Kris says to me from behind me as we get through the door.

"You're fine, sweetheart. We've got all day."

"Oh yeah, sure." She rolls her eyes. "Like you want to spend all day in a bookstore with me."

"I think you underestimate the things I would do to just be in your atmosphere."

She says nothing back to that. I see her smile though.

She goes ahead of me now that we are in here. Every now and then she will stop at a shelf. There has to be over a hundred shelves in this space. She runs her fingers over the spines of almost every one she goes by. Her nails are painted a shiny white right now and I am damn near mesmerized by the way she trails them across each book.

I am jealous of fucking books.

I huff a laugh and Kris turns her head to look over her shoulder. She is so damn cute. I just smile and wave and she laughs at me. By the time she is done perusing, she tells me that she did not find anything that called to her, so we leave empty handed.

"You really didn't see any you liked?" I ask as we hold hands and walk to the next little store she has on her mental list.

"Nothing I needed or really wanted. Cameron and I stopped at the bookstore in Kearney last week and I went a little hard. Surprised you didn't notice the new books on your shelf."

"Oh, I noticed. I ordered another shelf to match before we left for here."

She stops walking and I am yanked back to where she is frozen.

"You okay, babe?"

"You ordered another bookcase?"

Her question catches me by surprise. I didn't think it was anything to really write home about.

"Well," I rub the back of my neck. "I didn't think you'd want to have to stack your books all weird as you got new ones. Like, for aesthetic purposes or whatever."

She launches herself at me, almost knocking me into the parking meter behind me, throwing her arms around my neck. I wrap mine around her waist and pull her to me.

"I'll buy you a hundred bookcases if it makes you this happy, sweetheart."

And I mean it. I would.

"I'll let you know if I am in need of a hundred more." She giggles as she pulls away, but I don't let her go far. "Thank you. That was so considerate and kind of you, Carter. I'm not surprised but just," she pauses and smiles. "I'm just so damn happy."

I kiss her, hard and long, not giving a damn who sees us in the middle of the sidewalk.

Though maybe I should have.

"Kris?" a voice I don't recognize, but immediately dislike the sound of her name on, calls from behind me.

Kris freezes, but not in a cute way like a moment ago. This is like a new deer caught in headlights. I am pretty sure she is *shaking*. I turn around and see a man who I instantly hate. Light blonde hair, weird mustache that looks like he is trying too hard to be cool, a bright orange flannel that makes my eyes hurt, and the most obnoxious pair of Ray Bans I have ever seen.

On anyone else, all of that would probably be fine. But him... Nah.

"Michael," Kris finally says on an exhale and my head snaps to hers. She isn't looking back at me though. She is staring at him—

Michael. The man that treated her like she was damaged goods. Tears start to line her eyes. I step in front of her, putting myself between the two of them and looking at her. My hands go to her face and her eyes go to mine.

"Sweetheart, what do we do here? You lead, I follow. Remember? Okay?"

She nods.

"Give me words, honey."

"Okay," she says quietly. "I just want to say hi, I think. Yeah?"

"Whatever you want Kris." I kiss her forehead before turning back around and moving next to her.

Michael scratches the top of his head and looks at me quickly before looking back at Kris.

"Michael, hi." Her voice is steady, and the tears are gone. "How are you?"

His eyes widen slightly, and he shoves his hands into his jean pockets. "Yeah, uh, I'm, uh, I'm good."

Mumbling idiot.

I hold back my eye roll and squeeze Kris' hand.

"How are you?" he finally gets out.

With zero hesitation Kris says, "I'm good. Really good." She motions to me with her free hand. "This is my boyfriend. Carter this is Michael."

I take a step forward and stretch out my right hand. "Michael," I say with next to zero enthusiasm.

He takes my hand in his and gives it a slight shake. I would rate it a three out of ten if I had to.

I hate this guy.

"Spending Thanksgiving with John and Pen?" Michael asks.

"Yeah, we did. We go home tomorrow." She gives him a polite smile.

"Home? You don't live here anymore?" He looks so confused, and I am loving it.

Kris looks over at me and smiles. "Nope, I live in Nebraska now. With Carter and his son Cameron."

"Oh, wow, that's-"

I cut him off because I am over him and his slow-paced conversational skills. "Cool?" His eyes dart to mine. "Yeah, it is very cool that she's found a home with me. I'm a lucky son of a bitch." I pull her into my arm and kiss the top of her head. "We better get going though, Matthew."

"Micha-"

"See ya, Martin." I give him a little punch to his bicep as we pass. Kris's laugh fills my ears, my soul, as she turns her face into my side.

"You jealous, silly man."

"He's a dick and I was over it."

"Fair," she laughs. "I love you."

"I love you back, sweetheart."

Chapter Twenty-Four

Right Now The Best

Kris

"Oh, look at these, honey." I pull Carter over to the little plastic rack of bracelets. "You want to wear matching friendship bracelets with me?" I pick up a beaded neon green one.

"I absolutely want to do that with you," he says with zero hesitation. "You pick mine, I pick yours. Yeah?"

I look at him and smile. How did I get so lucky with him?

When we ran into Michael, I thought for sure I was going to break. And I almost did. But then Carter was in front of me, his hands on my face, and the tears vanished. The hurt disappeared. It turns out, I no longer give a fuck about Michael or his thoughts and opinions.

"Deal."

Neither of us shows the other which one we chose. I walked away and let him pick first and then he went and found a t-shirt for Cameron. We checked out, the both of us handing the cashier our bracelets in closed fists and with closed eyes. The gal behind the counter laughed and I just smiled like the lovesick idiot I am.

"Let's go next door to the coffee shop and then do the bracelet thing," I say as I grab his free hand. His other one is holding our bag from the shop we just left.

We order our drinks and sit down. This shop is one of my favorite places to work and read. Or *was* I suppose. Now my favorite places to work and read are in Nebraska on a farm.

"You know what we should get for the house?" I ask Carter as we sit down, drinks steaming in front of us.

"A puppy for Cam for Christmas?"

I laugh and look up at him, finding him to be stone cold serious.

"Oh," I say. "Well, let's circle back to that." He laughs an okay. "I was thinking a bench of some kind, or a comfy couch or swing, for the porch at home. The one that's up is nice but it feels so old and it's not super comfortable. I just picture sitting there after working in the mornings, taking a break with an iced coffee and a book or my Kindle. Cameron snuggled up with me on Saturday's while you check cows, and we don't want to put shoes on. That kind of thing." I shrug my shoulders, feeling a little silly now that I have said it aloud.

"Well, I've never heard of something we needed so badly." He smiles at me over his coffee. "Porch-swing-couch-thing, it is, sweetheart."

Knowing Carter the way I do, which is well at this point, this will not be some simple swing. Oh no, this will be the porch swing of my dreams.

About halfway through our drinks I remember our new jewelry.

"Let's do our bracelet thing!"

He pulls his tiny little plastic baggy out of his pants pocket and smiles widely. I grab mine out of my small purse.

Carter says, "Let's close our eyes and open a hand. Then we can both set each other's in the open hand. Yeah?"

I nod enthusiastically. I love a good surprise present. We both smile at each other, Carter winks at me, and we close our eyes.

The feel of his hand grazing mine as he places the jewelry there sends a shiver through my body and I hum out loud.

"Ready?" he asks quietly, his hand covering mine and my other one covering his.

"Ready."

It is such a small thing, a little beaded bracelet that did not even cost ten dollars. I still gasp though, clutching my specially chosen just-for-me bracelet to my chest and smiling at the man that loves his just as much.

"I love it!"

"It's perfect!"

We both speak at the same time and then laugh. Carter slides his over his hand, spinning it around his wrist. I do the same, admiring it with a smile.

"Yellow made me think of you," I say when I look back up at Carter, feeling just a little embarrassed. "Because you're so warm and good."

Carter smiles like I told him I want to buy him a new tractor, and my embarrassment melts away.

"I got you a red one because Nebraska is your home now," Carter says proudly. "And as such, red has to be in your daily wear."

"Yes, absolutely," I say. I get up and walk around the little table, leaning down and pressing a kiss to Carter's lips. "Yes, it is my home."

Carter brings a hand to the side of face and deepens the kiss and I don't even seem to care that we are in public, in a crowded coffee shop, on a busy day. No, all I can bring myself to focus on is the man kissing me here and the feeling he leaves in my soul.

"Dad, you can't get in the car and come with us. But you can fly down at any point and stay with us."

"We've got a room just for you, John. Any time."

My dad climbs out of the backseat. I am perplexed at how he even got in since it is stacked with random boxes of my stuff. Dad claps Carter on both shoulders before pulling him into a great big hug.

"Come back anytime, son. Love you."

My heart can't handle this. But I watch anyways. I watch as Carter squints his eyes, hugging my dad back with just as much fervor. Carter sniffles and pats my dad on the back.

"Yeah, love you too John. Thanks for," his voice cracks and my body fights the urge to join their embrace. "Thanks for everything."

They pull apart and smile at one another before my dad turns to me.

"Love you, kid." He hugs me tightly, but for a far less amount of time than just spent hugging my boyfriend. I can't even find it in me to mind.

"I love you too, dad. I'll call you."

"Don't forget about us," Bryce calls from the doorway.

"Never could, Bryce."

"It's true honey. You're unforgettable." Sherry is so serious about that, and it grosses me out how much she loves my brother. In a cute way.

Hugs are exchanged between everyone, my mom following shortly after Sherry and Bryce.

"I'm proud of you, honey," my mom whispers into my ear.

My eyes sting and I hug her extra tight.

"Thanks, mom. I love you."

"Love you too, Kris." She places a kiss on my forehead and hugs Carter.

Carter gets in the passenger side, letting me drive first because I like the first part of the drive. We wave out our open windows, the cold and crisp air swirling my hair around my face. Once we're down the street we roll them up and Carter takes my hand in his.

His hand covers mine over the gear shift and we stay like that for a while. I sing along with the music I hand selected. A lot of Zach Bryan and Taylor Swift. Carter goes between messing around on his phone and looking around. Cameron called us twice already to see when we would be home. Sadie said yes to us picking him up on the way through and keeping him an extra night. I speed a solid five over the speed limit almost always. Today I'm pushing eight over.

I miss that kid so damn much.

"Should we discuss the whole puppy for Christmas thing?" I ask after a beautiful rendition, in my opinion, of "I'll Call Your Mom" by Noah Kahan.

"Oh yeah, definitely. Let's get a puppy for us and Cam for Christmas, yeah?" Carter puts his phone down on the dash.

"Okay, sure. But puppies are a lot of responsibility. And I definitely want to do a rescue situation."

"Couldn't agree more. There's a shelter in Kearney that we could visit. I do want a puppy though, a rescue puppy I mean. And I know they're a lot of work but between the three of us we can do it. I think." He laughs and grabs my hand.

"Okay, puppy for Christmas then. Do we let Cameron pick the name?"

"He'd be crushed if we don't."

"Want to bet on whether he'll try to name it 'Dine-saur'?"

We both laugh and before I know it, we're halfway home.

Home.

I have had homes before. I still have the home I grew up in, my parents' home. I had built a home with Michael, albeit briefly, while we were together, and things were good. I even considered the little cabin in Alma home after the first week. But none of them had Carter or Cameron.

Home is not any of those places. Home is those boys.

My boys.

Chapter Twenty-Five

Without You

Carter

I have never been one to participate in ugly sweater contests or parties. It's not as though I dislike them. I attend them yearly, usually with Ken and one of his many plus-ones. I just don't do the whole dressing up thing. I do not judge those that do. It has never been something I had any desire to do, though.

But I tell you what. When Kris Katherine Atwater asks, with the perfect ass and the most beautiful thick hair that I have a sick obsession of running my fingers through whenever I get the chance— The woman that loves my son like he is her own and holds my heart in the palm of her beautifully manicured hand— I would sell my favorite pickup for that woman. Wearing a piece of clothing that makes her smile is literally the least I can, and will, do. I would get her damn name tattooed on my forehead if she asked.

Actually...

I shake my head, tucking away the idea of a tattoo for now.

"You ready, baby?" Kris yells from the bathroom.

The bathroom where she is literally the one we are waiting on. I roll my eyes and laugh.

"Sure am, honey!" her mom yells back in jest from the living room.

I can feel Kris roll her eyes and I smother a laugh at her expense.

Penny and John came down on a whim two days ago to stay for a full week. They were across the Nebraska state line before they called Kris and told her their plans. I choked on a laugh then too as she damn near yelled "You couldn't even wait a full month, mother?" But, I *had* told John about the spare room that is theirs if they ever want it. I'm happy to have them here. They met Cameron yesterday and everyone has been absolutely head over heals from the beginning.

"Yes, sweetheart. I'm ready."

"Okay, give me," she taps something onto the counter. "Like, fifteen minutes!"

I laugh again and go to stand in the bathroom. I lean my side on the frame of the door, crossing my arms over my chest. My yellow bracelet gets caught on a string of tinsel and I can't help but laugh at myself as I look in the mirror.

"Kenny is going to shit when he sees me in this thing."

John barks out a laugh from down the hall as he passes by to go to the couch. Kris looks at me in the mirror and smiles. Her hand that is holding the brush part of her mascara is halfway to her eye and she giggles.

"It's cute. He'll be jealous."

No, he will not be. But I don't tell her that. I will not suck the fun out of this for her.

"You look cute while you do that."

She pauses the stick at her eyelashes and narrows her eyes at me.

"Don't make fun. No one looks good applying this shit."

"You do."

She does. Her face is almost touching the mirror over the sink. Her eyes are wide, and her mouth is forming the perfect 'O' shape. I can't help that other things come to mind over that sight, but I push them aside. We do not have the time, to my major disappointment.

"Okay," she yells, startling me out of my dirty thoughts. "Ready!"

She pulls me to stand in front of the mirror with her. We are quite the pair. She is fucking gorgeous. These damn sweaters are just hilarious.

Kris has some torn up light blue jeans on and her cow print Hey Dudes. Her hair is curled the way she likes it, and she would say she is having a "good eyelash day" because she definitely is. Her sweater is the most outrageous shade of puke green. Think The Grinch but like, mushed peas. There are white Grinch-like hands perfectly placed on her chest, near her collarbone. They are each dangling bright red Christmas ornaments.

Over her tits.

It is distracting and I am going to have to try hard to not pay attention to anyone that looks at her *"ornaments"*. Covering the rest of her sweater are little bells, silver and gold, that are fully operational.

I fucking love this girl.

My sweater is a wreck. It is literally like Christmas threw up on me. Dark blue with little spots of green, red, and gold tinsel sewn throughout the entire thing. I too have been blessed with fully functional bells, mine silver, in the spots where the tinsel is not covering fabric.

But Kris handmade these bad boys and so even though I know I look like a moron— I am the luckiest moron in the state of Nebraska.

We walk to the living room, hand in hand, to say goodbye to her parents and Cameron. We find them all snuggled up on the couch. John has a book in one hand with a leg crossed over his knee. His other arm is stretched across the back of the couch and Cameron is settled right into John's side. Penny is sandwiching Cam in on the other side, twirling a small piece of his dark hair around her finger. It's about his bedtime, so his little eyelids are half-closed while he watches the end of *Monsters, Inc.*

I lean down over the back of the couch while Kris goes to the front of it. Kissing Cameron on the top of his head, I whisper, "I love you, bud. Be good for pop and nan."

Kris was adamant about not making Cameron feel like he's "being forced to have all of these new people in his life." But he took right away to calling John and Penny by their new names. They came up with them together last night. Kris watched the whole exchange while chewing on the inside of her lip like she does when she's nervous. But I soaked it all in. How lucky are Cameron and I to have gained a whole family to love, and to love us back.

"Luh you," Cam whispers back. "Luh you, Kiss."

Kris leans in and plants a kiss on Cameron's forehead. "Love you too, Camy."

We say goodbye to Kris's parents and make our way to the pickup. I pull Kris to a stop at the hood and wrap her in my arms.

"I love your parents. And I love how much they love Cameron." I kiss her lips.

"I know. I just worry about him being overwhelmed. But he really does seem to love them back, huh?" She smiles softly. Her fingers pull at the hem of my sweater. "I'll chill out, I promise. Finding the new dynamic with them is just going to take some give from me. I know I need to relax about it all. I will."

"It's all fine, sweetheart. Everyone loves everyone, right?" She nods. "Then there's nothing to worry about. So long as we've got that, we've got it all."

We kiss some more and my fake irritation with Kris' need to be punctual grows while I pout about the lack of time we have for anything else.

Once in the pickup and buckled, pulling out of the drive, Kris says quietly, "They really do make great grandparents, huh?"

I know how new that sentence must feel on her tongue.

I slide my hand under her thick hair and settle it on the back of her neck. My thumb sweeps across one of my favorite spots there and I say, "Yeah, sweetheart, they do."

The bar in Wilcox is the quintessential small-town bar. The owners are a brother and sister. Their parents help run things, as do their spouses. They are wholesome and good people, and they throw the best parties this side of the Platte.

I have a bottle of Busch Light in one hand and my other holds Kris's while she sips on her Malibu and pineapple drink in a dewy red plastic cup. A bright pink and a neon green straw poke out the top and every now and then she will absentmindedly stir her drink with them. She doesn't use them to drink. "They're too tiny to do much," she said earlier when I asked.

She has been through about five of those bad boys and my girl is starting to sway a bit. I bite back a laugh at the thought. I have never seen her beyond a little buzzed but here she is, tipping into almost drunk territory, and the cutest damn thing in this bar.

"Thinking we should head on home, sweetheart," I whisper in her ear. My lips brush her cheek, and she leans in and hums.

"We can't leave yet," she whisper-shouts. "I signed up for karaoke!"

Ken barks out a laugh, startling his bottle-blonde date that I don't even remember the name of.

I love Ken, obviously. There is just no denying that he gets around. So, I usually don't make a point to try very hard with his "friends". He has never minded my lack of effort, so I don't think about it much.

"Shut your big mouth. She can sing like a damn angel, Ken."

Kris laughs at me and pats my knee before squeezing it.

"No, I can't," she says between giggles. "But I'm going up there anyway, so prepare yourselves to be serenaded."

I love listening to her sing. She won't be winning any awards any time soon, but she would make it through first round auditions. Her voice is my favorite out there.

I hear the guy in charge of karaoke calling Kris's name. She smiles at me widely, shimmies her shoulders as she climbs down from the barstool, and winks at Ken while she plants a big ol' kiss on my cheek.

"Go get 'em, baby!" I yell as she swaggers off.

The old saying "I hate to see her go, but I love to watch her leave" springs to mind.

She really is beautiful, always. But a little flush to her cheeks from the booze and the warm atmosphere, the way her smile shines under the blue lights by the stage, and the fact that her eyes never leave mine... I would drop to one knee right now if I knew she would say yes.

The microphone cuts to Kris and she says, "I dedicate this song to my favorite person. My best friend. The biggest surprise of my life." She smiles and I just know her eyes hold some unshed tears. Mine would too if I weren't surrounded by people that would hassle me endlessly over it. "Without you, I wouldn't be so damn happy, honey. I love you."

I smile and yell, "I love you too, sweetheart!"

Kris giggles and the music starts. She doesn't even need the screen in front of her with the lyrics. She has been singing this song under her breath, and then not so under her breath, for the last four days. "Without You" by Diplo and Elle King has been a staple in our house as of late.

I do not know if it does in reality, but for me the room goes quiet. She is all I see. All I hear. Everyone fades away and it's like we are in a damn romantic comedy movie. It is taking everything in me to stay seated and not just grab her, toss her over my shoulder, and take her to our home to show her just how much control I simply don't have when it comes to loving her.

I don't look away from her the entire time. She is tapping her hand on her thigh along with the beat. Her eyes are closed, and her head is turned a little to the ceiling. Her painted red lips are so close to the microphone I am almost envious of the damn thing.

I am completely entranced.

"She's good," Ken says from across the table.

"She's perfect." I stand up as she finishes the song, her eyes connecting to mine. "I'll call you tomorrow, Kenny."

He just laughs and his girlfriend says goodnight, but I hardly hear them. All I hear is Kris laughing as she throws her arms around my neck and kisses me in this crowded bar, in these stupid sweaters that I will never throw away. The bells sound off as we shake with laughter and happiness. She kisses me like the very oxygen I am breathing is exactly what she needs to keep her standing upright.

"Let's go home," she whispers against my lips.

Chapter Twenty-Six

Santa Baby

Kris

"The party was a week ago, Kris. You can't still be hungover."

"I don't know how it's scientifically possible, Carter. But I'm telling you, I think I should never drink again. At least not in excess. I still feel like I am dying. Do I smell like booze?" I put my neck in his face where he is sitting on the couch. "Because I think it's still coming out of my pores." I am being so whiny still, a whole week after the party at the bar in town.

My parents left a couple of days ago and if I were to be fully honest with everyone, myself included, I am being extra dramatic because I kind of already miss them and that feeling is sort of new. I always miss my mom and dad in small amounts. But now that things have shifted slightly in how they look at me and treat me, and in the way they love Carter and Cameron... I really was sad to see them go.

I vaguely remember singing to Carter a week ago though, in front of dozens of people. I don't know how I did not miss a word during my very own shining star moment but I am claiming that brag and owning that shit.

And I am also never drinking again. Twenty-seven-year-old Kris simply can't hang like twenty-two-year-old Kris could.

Carter indulges me by sniffing at my neck. Even though I have showered several times between then and now, I am still expecting him to tell me I smell like coconut liquor. He doesn't though. Instead, he promptly runs his scruffy chin all over my exposed skin.

"If you make me laugh any more, I am going to perish. Right here, Carter. Dead. Deceased. Rest in peace, me."

"You're so cute when you're being so dramatic."

He lightly slaps my hip as I straddle his lap, then runs his hand over the spot there and down my leg.

It's the day after Christmas, and we get Cameron this afternoon and then until the second day of January. Sadie and Lance have had him for the last week, he went to their house the day after the party at the bar. And while I love that for them, I miss the kid something fierce. But it has also been nice to spend some one-on-one time with Carter at home during such a down time.

Carter only gave me a day of whining and properly lazing about before he kicked back into full Farm Daddy gear. We have checked cows together, changed the oil in his little Kabota tractor and in the grain cart's tractor. Carter got my newest bookcase set up. I immediately organized all of my books that needed a home, and got other special little things situated just so on it. We have watched the entire Santa Clause franchise and then followed it up with the Home Alone's. I baked him so many cookies that I swear at one point I saw his eyes droop at the fresh plate of chocolate chip ones. So, I am on a self-imposed ban from baking for the foreseeable future. We have played a few games of Yahtzee and spent quite a bit of time in bed, loving each other irrevocably. It has been the most wonderful Christmas I have ever had. And, with Cameron being at his mom's for a whole week, we had the perfect opportunity to go find us a puppy.

She is fifteen weeks old, and the softest, buttery yellow, fluffy golden retriever mix I have ever seen. She is unnamed and almost fully house trained already. Her eyes are ice blue, from whoever the dad is, and they melt my heart every time she looks at me. Her mom was a stray and got pregnant and taken to the shelter. I'm not really a dog person, admittedly. I don't dislike them, but I do not *need* them.

I *need* Puppy though. That is what we have called her thus far. She is perfection. Cameron is going to be so pumped when he gets here later today.

I pick my head up off of Carter's shoulder and bring my lips to his brow. His face is burrowed deep into my chest and I can't help but laugh.

"Shhh," he says. "I'm sleeping."

"You're a dork." I move to get up, but Carter's arms fly to my waist and hold me to him. "Carter, we have to get Puppy put away before Cam gets here. Come on, up up."

"Okay fine. But I'm coming back to this very spot, right here, tonight." He looks up at me, his blue eyes crinkled at the corners and stark against his tan skin. "Got it?"

I laugh and sigh, feigning exasperation. "Got it."

Not a second too soon did we get Puppy squared away because the second she is in Cameron's bedroom and quiet, my favorite little almost-three-year-old is bouncing through the front door with so much excitement, I swear the house shakes.

"Cam man!" Carter meets him halfway and I stay put on the couch.

I can be overwhelming, so I often like to let Cameron get in the house fully before I love on him too much.

"Dad!" Carter picks Cameron up and swings him around. His little arms go tight around Carter's neck, and they embrace each other for a while. Sadie leans against the doorframe and smiles.

"Merry Christmas, Barker family," she says cheerily.

Don't hate the way that sounds, me being included in that, not one bit.

"Merry Christmas, Sades. Lance stay home?"

"Yeah, he wanted to shower before we go to Omaha."

Sadie walks over to where I am on the couch and leans down to hug me.

"Merry Christmas, Sadie. Did you have a good one?"

"The best," she says wistfully before throwing her left hand in front of my face. My gaze snaps to the massive solitaire diamond taking up the majority of her small knuckle.

"Holy shit!" I get up and hug her tightly. "Holy shit!"

We jump together, holding on for dear life and laughing. I am not entirely sure when it happened, but Sadie has become one of my best friends. We text constantly. She invites me to random things like book club and meal club and whatever other clubs small towns can think of. And I almost always go. We have lunch dates and coffee dates, and she will come hang out with me at home even if both Cameron and Carter are out and about. We have our own little relationship, and she makes me feel so welcome not only in this family, but in this town.

"You're engaged!"

We still have not stopped jumping.

"I am!"

We squeal a few more times before stopping finally and looking at Carter and Cameron. They are frozen, looks of absolute amusement on their faces, and laughter nearly choking them.

"Congrats Sades. Glad Lance finally locked your ass down." Carter hugs Sadie tight.

"Thanks buddy. You can be one of the flower boys for me, yeah?"

"Absolutely not." He ruffles her brown ponytail. "But I'll obviously be there."

"Well duh. Kris is going to be a bridesmaid." Sadie winks at me.

Cameron whips his little head to where I am standing, still in his dad's arms, and shouts, "Kissy!" at the top of his small lungs.

"Camy!" I hold my hands out and he all but lunges out of Carter's arms.

"Miss you, Kissy," he says into my nose as he gives me the wettest toddler kisses.

"Buddy, I missed you so dang much."

We stay that way, his mouth basically sealed to the bridge of nose and my eyes closed, as we sway back and forth slightly. When I open my eyes, I look up to see Sadie with one hand on her neck under her chin and her other crossed beneath her chest. She has red cheeks and glassy eyes and a smile so soft and sweet it damn near makes me cry too. And then there is Carter. Carter with the black stubble that he refuses to shave because he likes to run it over any and all exposed skin I have at any moment. Carter with the blue eyes that are not holding his tears at bay. Carter, the man I love with my entire heart and soul.

We all say nothing for a moment as Cameron snuggles his head into the crook of my neck. I rub his back and continue to sway.

"I love you guys," Sadie says finally, breaking the silence. "Like, a whole lot."

She leans in and kisses Cameron on the cheek before doing the same to me.

"I love you too," I whisper.

"Luh you mama," Cameron whispers, following suit and saying it softly.

"Yeah, love you too Sades." Carter follows her to the door and closes it behind her. He makes his way back over and takes both Cam and I into his arms.

Safe. Warm. Loved. Cherished. Whole.

And then it all goes to hell in the most delightful way as Cameron hears Puppy scratch at his bedroom door, yipping loudly.

Chapter Twenty-Seven

Temporary Town

Carter

I have never been the real down in the dumps type. I've never really had a time in my life where I had this yearning for better, for more. I got dealt a shitty hand with my parents passing away so early in my life, but I did what I had to do and grieved in a way that worked for me. I don't have a lot from them, they just did not have much to begin with. But what I do have are small things like random photos of them as kids or when they were together. Some of the three of us when I was small. And my most prized possession; my dad's vinyl collection.

It's only about two dozen records. Some ABBA, Simon and Garfunkel, Pink Floyd. I have always wanted to get a record player but just never got around to it. It had just never been something that had weighed heavy on my mind to get done. So, his records have always had their home on my bookcase by the television and that had been that.

Kris must have noticed, like she does. I remember her asking if I had a record player when she was dusting one day about a month or so ago. I told her no, that the records were my dad's, and they are just there to be there. She hummed in answer and that was that.

Except it wasn't. Because this woman gifted me the most incredible record player for Christmas. I don't know any of its specifications, but I do know that it is perfect and "Bridge Over Troubled Water" by S&G has never sounded better in my life.

Right now, though, Cameron in bed with Honey the puppy, and the house suitably messed up after Christmas shenanigans, "Temporary Town" by Charles Wesley Godwin is playing softly from where my new present is sitting in the middle of the dining room table.

I have Kris in my arms, one hand holding hers to my chest and the other playing with the hem of her white t-shirt. I'm running a finger over the bright red nail polish she's got on, and she has her head turned and resting on my chest. We are swaying back and forth, her humming along to the song and me singing it softly in her ear. I don't let many people hear that— me singing. It is *not* good. But for some insane reason, Kris loves it when I sing to her. I can't seem to not do anything she loves.

"I love you," she whispers.

"Sweetheart," I say back. "I love you so damn much."

"Marry me" echoes in my brain a few times before we go back to humming and singing.

I want to ask her. I want to drop to my knees and fucking beg the woman. I yearn to say those words. But she is still finding herself, my girl. And I will be damned if I fuck that up. So, I wait. I will not wait forever though— we all know this. She would say yes right now, I am almost positive. But I don't want her to feel like that is what she *has* to do for me. Not that she would not want to marry me, but I don't want her to feel like it is "what's supposed to be done" now. It has only been a few months, I know, but it has been years for me, in my soul.

So, I will wait a little longer. Get us through the holidays and the new year, and maybe Valentine's Day. But then it is game on.

"Hey, you sure you don't want to come with us?" I ask Kris as I get ready to go meet Sadie and Lance for a late lunch and drink. "We can drop Cam off with Sadie's aunt on the way."

"I'm okay, really. I think I'm peopled out after the holidays and having my parents here. Sorry."

I walk over to where Kris is standing in the kitchen. Her back to the counter by the coffee maker and a sparkly green mug Sadie got her from Starbuck's in hand.

"Don't be sorry, honey. It's fine. Tell Cam to take it easy on you then, yeah? You two can nap or something."

I press a kiss to her lips and then her forehead before turning around to find and say goodbye to my kid.

"It's so nice out in the sun, I think we might go make use of my new couch swing." She winks at me.

That couch-swing is the best thing I have ever made with my own two hands. And Kris has let me know how much she appreciates the "masterpiece" as she puts it, damn near every night. It did not take me but a couple weeks. I built it in the garage that Kris never uses even though I constantly ask her to. It is the most beautiful shade of cherry walnut, and it's deep enough that her and I could both lay down on it fully. It's long enough for that too. And yes, that was all intentional. I had Sadie help me pick out some real nice white and pink floral cushions for it. Even got Kris some dark green pillows and a little white knitted blanket.

I find her sometimes just looking at the damn thing. Like she can't believe it's hers. I would build her a thousand of them if it made her happy like that. And if we had somewhere to put them all.

"Love you, sweetheart."

"I love you back, Carter. Have fun."

I turn back around, stopping at the door. She just looks at me over her coffee and smiles softly.

"What?" she asks.

I shake my head. "I don't know." And I don't. I don't know why I feel the need to pause and take her in. "Just soaking it all in, I think."

Her smile grows and she sets her cup down before striding over to me. Her fuzzy red socks over her black leggings make it look like she is gliding across the hardwood floor. When she reaches me, she grabs the front of my red sweatshirt and pulls me to her.

"I love you very much Carter Arlington Francis." She kisses me and it makes me want to take my boots off and stay home. "Bring me back a vanilla latte?" Kris rubs her nose against mine. "I love you, stud."

I fucking love her so much. So, I am not entirely sure what this pinch in my chest is all about right now as I tell her goodbye again.

The weird feeling does not settle though, as I pull into the restaurant to meet Sadie and Lance. I push through, but I can't help but wonder what this ache is all about.

Chapter Twenty-Eight

Set Fire to the Rain

Kris

I can't wait to thank Carter tonight for this massive porch swing— *again*. I have never felt as seen and heard as I did when he blindfolded me on Christmas morning and walked my all-too happy ass out onto the porch to show me this masterpiece. He built it with his own two hands. Found the plans online and then made it extra-large so that he could lay with me, so that Cameron could hang out here too with me, or Carter, or the both of us, when it is quiet time. It has the most beautiful cushions. They give old Victorian vibes, and the blanket and pillow are the perfect additions. The whole thing is epic and nearly indescribable.

Currently I have my book open, and a glittery green travel mug filled with "vanilla creamer and some coffee" as Carter would say. He built in little divots in the armrests on this swing so that we could set any sort of drink or food in there without worrying about it sliding off or bouncing around. Carter thought of it all.

I love that man.

Cameron is inside the house, just on the other side of the front door. I can see him from here. Carter made sure to put the swing in right where it is so that we can watch Cameron play on the porch, or in the living room, or in the front yard. I just looked over my shoulder a second ago and he was laying on his tummy, his little ankles crossed and in the air, with his dinosaurs and tractors in front of him.

I laughed.

Dinosaurs farming, what a thought.

I am about halfway through *When We Were* by Diana Elliot Graham. My heart is racing at what's going on in this wonderfully written story. That's when I hear it— The most guttural, heart stopping noise. I have never moved so fast in my life. I am up and off the swing in what feels like no time and I am sliding through the front door on my sock-clad feet across the wooden floor.

"Cameron?" My voice comes out nearly breathless. "Cam?!"

I hear his crying from the other side of the couch and bolt towards the noise. My heart is in my throat and my brain is going a million miles a minute.

Did I forget to blow the candle out and he burned himself?
I didn't have any candles lit.

Did he step on a random nail somehow?

How would there be a nail in here?

Did the television fall on top of him?

It is bolted to the fucking wall, Kris.

I round the couch and find Cameron curled into a ball with big tears running down his face. There is blood everywhere. Like, *everywhere*. On his blue and gray striped t-shirt. On his face, in his hair, on the floor.

"Cam!" I drop to the floor and take a deep breath. He is a wreck, he doesn't need me to be one too. "Baby, what happened? Show me what's wrong."

He takes a big deep gasp and moves his hand from his face. I feel like I can almost see his brain through the gash on his forehead.

My hands fly to my mouth before I remind myself to stay calm. "Oh gosh," I whisper. "Honey, we're going to put a towel on there and we're going to go see a doctor, okay?" I pull my phone out of my pocket while I mutter, "what do I do, what do I do?" over and over again.

I pick Cameron up off the floor and carry him to the kitchen. He's not crying hysterically anymore but that just makes me nervous, and I am already out of my depth here.

"What the fuck do I do?"

I dial Carter's number and he picks up on the second ring.

"Hey sweetheart. Everything all good?"

I try to keep my voice calm, even though I am anything but. I do not know what the fuck I am doing here. They trusted me with this sweet, angel child and now he is bleeding out of his forehead, so much so that if I could collect it all it would be a good donor amount. And it is all because I was the one watching him.

"Carter. Cameron hurt his head and he's bleeding a lot and I think he needs stitches, and I don't know what to do." It comes out in a rushed whisper, so I don't freak out Cam more.

"Shit, alright." He sounds calm and not mad like I'm sure he is. "It's okay honey. Have him try to keep a towel pressed to his head, he might not and that's okay, but just tell him to and see what happens. Put him in the car and go to Holdrege. We'll meet you there, alright?"

"Yeah, yeah, okay." I pick up Cameron and make our way to the door. I don't even think about the fact that he does not have a coat on and neither of us have shoes on. "Carter." My voice cracks and the tears that I have been fighting come back with vengeance.

"Sweetheart, it's okay. I'm sure he's fine. Just breathe, baby. We'll see you in a few."

I don't fucking belong here.

That's the only thing, next to *"this poor sweet boy"* that keeps running through my brain. I am not meant for this. For this kind of life where there is a small child that is my responsibility. It doesn't matter that I want to be meant for that. That I yearn to have this life. I can't have children, and this feels like a sign as to why.

"I'm so sorry, Cameron," I whisper into his soft hair. I inhale deeply, soaking in everything that he is. "I'm so sorry."

He is looking at me like not a thing is wrong as I buckle him into his car seat.

"You are doing such a good job holding that on your head, buddy. We'll get you to your mom and dad, okay? It's all going to be fine."

"Okay Kissy." He smiles at me, but I don't feel deserving of that smile.

The hospital is a twenty-minute drive. I make it in fifteen. Safe but fast, I like to think.

We have seen the doctor. Carter, Sadie, and Lance are about five minutes out still and the nurse just brought in the things needed for stitches.

"Can you wait until his mom and dad get here?" I ask her.

She told me her name, but I have forgotten it, and I can't seem to take my eyes off the top of the little noggin that is pressed to my chest right now. Cameron is concussion free so when he yawned during the doctor's inspection, he said that if he needed to rest, he could. So, Cameron climbed right into my lap where I was sitting in a green recliner by the bed and snuggled in.

"Sure thing," she smiles and turns towards the door. Her bright blonde hair is in a tight ponytail, and it swishes around her small shoulders. "I'll be back in a few."

I don't say anything in response and instead just press a kiss to the top of Cameron's head.

"I'm so sorry Cameron. I'm so sorry." I sniffle and try to reign in the tears again.

The guilt is insurmountable. It is all consuming and drowning. This can't be a normal feeling for every parent when their child gets hurt, can it? Because this is fucking *painful.*

"I won't ever let something like this happen again, Cameron," I promise him quietly. "I'm so sorry."

The doctor got to asking Cam what had happened. Apparently, he had decided he wanted to see if he could fly, like his dinosaur that has the wings. So, in the short amount of time from the last moment I peeked in at him, he had climbed onto the back of the couch, taken the small blanket from there, spread it wide like wings, and dove off the damn thing. Upon landing, the noise of which got covered by his screaming, his head smacked down on a big, bright blue block that was left over from our morning of castle building.

The doctor called it "the perfect accident."

I call it "my fuck up."

Carter and Sadie rush through the door, their faces calm but their movements quick.

Sadie walks up to us and I go to give her Cameron, but she shakes her head and whispers, "It's okay. He's comfy. Let him rest."

She kisses his head and smiles at me. I wish she wouldn't do that— smile at me. I am why we are here.

I had texted Sadie, knowing she wouldn't be the one driving, and told her what happened while Cameron told the doctor and I.

"Are you okay?" she asks me.

I balk. "Me?" I all but shout. "I'm fine, Sadie. I'm just so sorry." Tears start to fall and now I worry that I won't be able to stop them this time. I look to Carter. "I'm so, so sorry."

"Oh honey," Carter whispers as he nears us.

Sadie at the same time says, "Kris, girlfriend."

I shake my head and close my eyes tightly. "I can't-"

"Mom and dad, I presume?" The blonde nurse comes in and everyone's attention shifts to her. Sadie and Carter nod and I give Cameron to him before standing and moving towards the door.

"I'm going to go wait with Lance." I say to no one in particular.

Sadie and Carter and Cameron all look at me, their faces soft and kind. Cam's is a little sleepy still. I got what I could of the dried blood off his face.

I don't wait for anyone to say anything before I walk out. I find Lance in the waiting room, messing around on his phone.

"How's he doing?" he asks me as I sit across from him.

"Fine." I swallow. "He's fine. A trooper."

"He's pretty great," Lance says and smiles at me before returning to his phone.

So, I sit here. In this small waiting room, in this small hospital, in this small town, feeling...

Small.

And feeling like I do not belong here at all.

Chapter
Twenty-Nine

What Hurts the Most

Carter

Sadie let Cameron choose where he wanted to sleep tonight and to my delight, he chose my house. I just got done tucking him in and reading to him. Lately it has been both Kris and I during bedtime, one at the foot of the bed and the other laying down with him. He picks every night who reads, and we do our thing. Tonight, it's different though.

Kris is not with me as I exit his room.

I close the door behind me after one last look at my boy. He is fine. He's tough and brave, and a total boy. Jumping off the back of the couch like that— mine for sure.

I shake my head and smile a little, sending Sadie the picture I took of him sleeping before I left. As I go to our room, mine and Kris's, my hands twitch with the anticipation of laying them on my girl.

She was pretty shaken. A lot distraught and a little quiet. She barely spoke, not to me or Sadie or Lance before we left the hospital. Hardly got close to Cameron but would not take her eyes of him. As though she thought he might break if she got too close. We went about our day, nursing our boy and just getting things cleaned up.

"Sweetheart," I say as I walk into our room. I immediately lose all focus on anything other than the open suitcase on the bed. "Going somewhere?" My voice is strained and my chest is tight. I put a fist to where I am sure my heart was once beating as I slowly look up at Kris.

Her emerald eyes are wide and lined with tears, some have fallen down her face. She gasps on a sob before turning back to her suitcase.

"Talk to me Kris. What's going on here?" I sound gentle but I am feeling anything but.

If she thinks I am going to let her walk out of here without some sort of fight, she is insane.

"I can't," she whispers as she zips the current bane of my existence.

"You need to." I cross the room and grab her wrists to stop her from picking up the stupid thing. "Please." I am not above begging. Not when it comes to Kris.

She pulls away from me and I am momentarily stunned. She has never pulled away from me, not *ever*. I know kids can be a lot, but she loves Cam. I know she does. I put my hands in my jean pockets and square my shoulders.

After a moment of silence, Kris staring at the silver band on her index finger and my staring at her face, I say, "Dime for what's on your mind, sweetheart? Give me something here. Anything." I need to defuse this situation as quickly as possible.

She sniffles and shakes her head. "Don't call me that, Carter. Not now."

My eyes widen. My heart shows proof of life as it breaks slightly.

"Kris. I need to know what's going on. What happened?"

Her gaze shoots to mine and her eyes narrow. She throws her arms up and almost yells, "Carter! Cameron had to get twelve fucking stitches today!" she drops her hands and I go to take a step towards her, but she holds one up to stop me. "It's my fault. I was supposed to be watching him. I was watching him!"

"Baby, I know you were. No one is questioning that."

She shakes her head. "But then why is he lying in bed right now with a massive gash in his head Carter? It's all my fault. I shouldn't be here. He deserves better than that— than me."

She sniffles and my entire body vibrates with the need to hold her. But something tells me she doesn't need that right now, or at least she thinks she doesn't.

She takes a deep breath, straightening her body and rolling her shoulders back. The tears are still rolling down her flushed cheeks, but she says calmly, "I shouldn't be here. I'm not meant to be here Carter. I'm going home."

I do not give a fuck about what she needs now. I move to her, one long stride and I am in her space, taking her face in my hands.

"Absolutely not."

Kris scoffs and rolls her eyes. "I wasn't asking Carter."

"Neither was I, Kris."

We have a stare off, neither of us blinking or moving except for my thumbs that swipe at her cheeks.

"This is your *home*, Kris." My voice is soft and quiet. "Sweetheart, *we* are your home."

I don't move first and when she does, I feel like I might be sick. She pulls out of my grasp and moves around me. I spin with her.

"Cameron deserves better, Carter. Today is proof that I am simply not meant for this." She waves her hand around. "All of the pregnancy issues and the damaged uterus and the broken me," she looks at me. "It's all proof that I am not meant to be this. Proof that Michael was right-"

"Do not tell me you actually believe that, Kris." My anger towards that dope is brewing and the panic over our current situation is not helping to keep it at bay.

Kris ignores me though.

"About it all. I shouldn't be an almost-mom or any sort of parent. And I can't lie to myself about that anymore. I need to leave before any of us are in too deep." I laugh desperately but she doesn't stop. "Cameron is young, by the time he's ten he won't even remember me. It's better for everyone if I go now."

She is a fucking lunatic, this woman.

"No." I shake my head. "*No.*"

"Carter-"

I invade her space again and cut her off, taking her hands in mine. She closes her eyes and hangs her head down.

"What do you need Kris? You need me to tell you that it's already too late and we are all in this too deep? Every one of us. Sadie, Cam, me. Fucking Lance even said how much he loves you today." I pull her to me and her head rests on my chest. "You need me to tell you that I love you more than I have ever loved anyone or anything in my entire life? That the kind of love I have for *our* son is neck and neck with the kind of love I have for you? You need the moon, Kris?" I shake my head and take her face in my hands, forcing her to look at me. "Open your eyes, honey. Look at me." She does. "Fuck the moon, I'll get you the sun. All you'd need to do is ask and it's yours. A life without you would be like a life without the sun. Without its warmth and light. That is what you are Kris. You are my warmth, my light." I press my brow to hers.

"But you'd get burned Carter. That's what I do. I burn things."

"Oh, sweetheart. I'm not scared of a little fire."

We stay like that, quiet and just breathing the same air. I start to think things have settled, but as she moves... I realize I may be a damn idiot today.

"It's not enough Carter." Kris steps away from me, out of reach.

No.

No no no no.

I walked away from her once. I cannot let her go again. I can't.

"Kris, please," I say. "Just, *please.*" I am about to drop to my fucking knees, but I don't honestly think it would do either of us any good at this point.

"I love you, Carter. I'm so sorry that Cameron got hurt."

"He's fine, Kris. He's okay, he's fine. I love you. Please, *sweetheart.*"

"I'm sorry." She goes around me, grabbing her suitcase. She pauses at the door, and I feel like I can't breathe. "I love him, okay? I love you. So much."

I tell my feet to move. I tell my mouth to refute her actions. I tell myself to fucking do something— *anything.* But then the front door is closing, and the noises are gone and my heart is in a fucking Toyota Camry on the way to Fargo, North Dakota.

My knees finally hit the floor then, the sharp pain in both doesn't even register. All I feel is the hole. The emptiness. That lack of light and warmth inside of me— inside of this house.

"*Fuck,*" I gasp as the tears of my own making fall around me.

Chapter Thirty

Be Happy

Kris

I hear my brother whisper, "Sherry, she hasn't showered in four days. She needs-"

Sherry hisses back, "She *needs* to grieve this relationship that she thought was end game, Bryce. She also needs support. Not lectures. Leave. Her. Alone."

"She also doesn't need hearing aids, in case you guys wanted to know that."

I turn my head to look over my shoulder. Bryce is leaning on the kitchen counter by the sink with his hands clasped in front of him, his knuckles nearly white. Sherry is next to him, mirroring his stance. Their eyes don't leave mine as their cheeks turn a little pink.

"Listen, Kris. I love you. You know that right? You're my sister, my *twin,* and I love you."

I face forward again, putting my focus— No, not focus, my gaze. I don't have any focus left in me right now. I put my gaze on the television. A Vanderpump Rules marathon is on BravoTV today and thank goodness for that because what else would I be mindlessly not paying attention to while I think about how broken and atrocious I feel? With that thought my eyes flit to little string of red beads resting snug against my wrist. I blink away my persistent and annoying tears, taking a deep breath. The irrational part of me wants to rip it off and throw it away. Watch as the tiny crimson circles scatter and bounce around this open space like the memories of Nebraska do in my empty chest and mind. But the larger, louder part of me, that is desperate to hold on to what I can from Nebraska and the life I was building there— Well, that sad bitch keeps the bracelet right where it is.

Two weeks. Two weeks have come and gone. Fourteen full days of the sun rising and setting and the moon coming out to mock me until it returns to its slumber. A slumber that I have been unable to join in on as of late.

And boy, does it show. The dark circles under my eyes, the dullness in my greasy hair, the chapped skin on my lips. I am a fucking disaster. And if my brother and Sherry think I am unaware of that fact, they would be mistaken.

I know. I am well aware that I am a depressed shell of what I was a mere fortnight ago. But what does anyone expect? I left the loves of my life two states south.

Do I regret it?

You bet.

Will I go back and put Cameron and Carter in harm's way because I clearly am not destined to have a family?

No.

So, here I will stay. Unbathed. Unhappy. And unable to want to do anything about it.

The couch shifts as Bryce sits next to me.

"I'm going to be the bad cop here, Kris. And I'm slightly sorry for it."

"Oh, goody." I roll my eyes.

Bitchy, much?

"You've got to get off of my couch and shower. Now. And then you need to get out of this house and go work for a few hours. Don't think we haven't noticed the lack of productivity around here. The last thing you need is to lose your job. And also, you need to eat. And drink some water. And just," Bryce takes a deep breath.

"Just *live*, honey," Sherry says from behind the couch, much softer. "We need you to just live again."

It is the sadness in her voice that does it for me. I don't say a word. I simply get up, numb, and make my way to the bathroom. It's like a robot has taken over and every move, every thought, is mechanical.

Close the door.

Turn on the shower.

Take off the clothes.

Start to cry.

Avoid looking in the mirror.

Get in the shower.

Do not turn the heat down, you deserve to fucking burn.

Continue to cry.

I go through the motions. I do the required things while bathing.

Once out of the shower, I brush my sad hair and then clean my gross teeth. I go about getting dressed in a pair of leggings that I can only hope are clean, and a long sleeve t-shirt. I was not paying attention to what I grabbed and when I looked down to make sure it wasn't stained, at least not in a major way, I start crying again.

My knees hit the floor and my hands cover my face as I sob.

"Kris, what happened?"

Bryce tries to pull my hands away while Sherry rubs soft circles on my back.

"I. Hate. This." I say between gasps.

"We know, sugar. We know."

The tears eventually settle and the gray shirt I got at the Nebraska Husker's football game with Carter is now soaked with them.

Fitting.

I haven't looked in a mirror or window yet since I got back up here, avoiding seeing the sad sack of shit I have become.

And who's fault is it?

Mine.

I only have myself to blame. I go over every reason why as I make my way to the coffee shop. A different one than the place Carter and I visited over Thanksgiving. I'm a masochist but I am not completely idiotic.

I tried to have a life that was not meant for me. Carter is too good, too pure, for me. Cameron is not my son— I can't have one of those. Even Sadie, she isn't my friend, she deserves better.

As I take a sip of the iced vanilla latte I ordered, like it was muscle memory, the words on my laptop blur and I close my eyes.

"Kris?"

Perfect. Just what I deserve.

"Kris?" he asks again while softly touching my shoulder.

I flinch and he pulls back. I force myself to look at him as he rounds the table and sits in the seat in front of me.

"Michael," I say coldly.

He does not hide the hurt in his eyes. He never was able to.

"I didn't realize you were back," he says.

"Why would you?"

"I guess that's fair." He runs his pale hand through his sandy colored hair.

He is the opposite of Carter in every way. Where Carter is tan and kind, Michael is pasty and unforgiving. Carter has the bluest, deep eyes. Michael has dark brown eyes that used to hold affection and love for me— Until it all turned to disappointment and resentment.

"You back for a quick visit?" he asks carefully.

Good. Fear me.

"Nope." I don't look at him, keeping my un-focused-focus on the screen of blurred letters and numbers.

Michael clears his throat and leans forward. "Listen, Kris... I owe you about a million and one apologies."

I look at him now, narrowing my eyes. He looks like he did the last time I saw him, when Carter and I ran into him downtown over Thanksgiving. He looks good. Happy. Healthy.

And here I am. Not any of those things. How unfair.

"Go ahead then. You won't hear me arguing about that."

"I am so sorry, Kris. I didn't realize how horrible I had been to you until I saw you last year again." He smiles softly. "That was the happiest I'd ever seen you. Since well, before everything"

"Before I couldn't stay pregnant, and you called me broken?" I blink at him and tilt my head.

His eyes grow wide. "Did I really say that to you?" His question is barely above a whisper.

I laugh, though it doesn't sound at all real. "Once. But you treated me that way every day after the third miscarriage." I look away and stare at the condensation on my clear plastic cup. "It's not my fault. I didn't break my body, Michael. I didn't miscarry on purpose. I wanted those babies." My voice breaks but I do not care. "I wanted those babies with *you*, Michael. I wasn't broken. I just wasn't lucky."

"No, I know. Damn, Kris, I know all of that." We lock our tear-filled eyes. "I'm so fucking sorry. I can't hardly remember that part of our lives, honestly."

"Lucky you."

"I just remember being so fucking *sad*. All the time. And mad. Gosh, I was mad Kris. I'm so sorry I hurt you. I'm sorry I made you grieve alone and go through shit that I physically and emotionally don't understand. I'm just so sorry." Tears are slowly trickling down his clean-shaven face. I watch one as it pools around the crease of his nose. "I am really sorry, Kris."

I take a deep breath and let his words sink in. Once upon a time I loved this man with everything I had. But even then, it wasn't like the love I have for Carter.

"I left him," I whisper.

He matches my volume as he asks, "Why?"

"His son, Cameron, is almost three and he's incredible." I swipe at the tears I do not deserve to cry over this. "I was watching him one day and he got hurt and it wasn't my direct fault, but I was there, Michael. And he got hurt. And it is my fault because I'm not meant to have kids and I tried to keep him anyways." The tears are flowing freely, and I do not think I have the energy to stop them even if I wanted to.

"You think you don't deserve to have that kind of life, Kris?" He sounds genuinely shocked.

"With my track record of trying to reproduce, I think it's pretty obvious that someone somewhere doesn't want me to have children."

"You got dealt a real shitty hand. We did. That's it. Don't let those losses keep you from gaining something real. You deserve to be happy. Damn, if anyone in this world deserves happiness, it's you, Kris." He smiles as his bottom lip wobbles.

"I loved you," I say.

"I loved you too," he says while squeezing my hand. "Go be happy, Kris. Don't punish yourself for shit you had no control over."

As Michael leaves, waving outside the large window I'm sitting next to, I breathe a little easier. I think about that, about what he just said to me.

"Be happy," I whisper to myself.

But how do I do that from here and after I already messed it all up?

Chapter Thirty-One

Come Back Home

Carter

I take off my hat and bend the gray bill between my dirt covered hands. My breath feels sharp, and my lungs feel too small. My chest aches and it is this persistent pain that will not go away.

Not that I want it to. I want to feel this pain. It is better than feeling nothing.

"Hey pal."

"Ken. Hey." My words come out flat. I turn around, putting my hat back on, and watch him walk out of my house.

"I stopped by to say hey, see how you're doing. You weren't here obviously when I got here so, figured I'd wait. Grabbed you a beer. You're welcome." He hands me a bottle.

"Thank you for bringing me one of my beers out of my fridge, Kenny. Appreciate it." I let the sarcasm fall.

I take a drink and make my way off the driveway and to the peeling white steps of the porch. I don't take my eyes off of the swing I built for Kris. But I don't sit in it either. No one has. Not for two weeks. I rub at my chest at the thought. The bracelet she gave me catches on the tiny pills of cotton on my shirt and I hesitate before looking at the yellow reminder. The reminder I do not need since all I think about is Kris and the fact that she isn't here.

"So," Ken says.

"So."

"What can I do here, man?"

I look up at that— at the somber tone of his voice. He is standing in front of me on the sidewalk, one hand running through his blonde hair and the other putting the bottle of beer to his lips.

"Nothing, bud. I'll be fine. Eventually."

Liar.

I'm fucking drowning here. I keep it together when Cameron is here but the questions from him still have not stopped.

Part of me hopes they never do.

"Where Kiss go?"

"Why leave?"

"She come back pease."

"I miss Kissy."

Every time I see him. Every call we have.

Sadie is sad too, missing her friend.

It is all fucking crushing.

"Don't lie to me, Carter. Not me. I get it. I know you're hurting. But what are you going to do about it?"

I raise my brows and ignore my drink. Everything tastes like trash now anyways.

"What do you mean? She left. I couldn't make her stay."

"But you could go get her back."

I tilt my head. "She. Left. I respect her, Kenny. I may not like that she's gone but what am I supposed to do? Fly to North Dakota, show up at what I am assuming is her brother's house, throw her over my shoulder, and drive her back down here? Force her to be here? Make her be a stepmom, a farmer's wife, the owner of some fucking chickens and cows?"

"Well, the chickens are probably optional." He shrugs and smiles and I want to hit him.

"Is this a fucking joke to you?" I demand, setting my beer down and standing up. "Am I a fucking joke to you?"

"Carter, obviously not. But I saw how much she-"

"She left!" I am yelling now, and I never yell. Not unless it is at one of my cows when they are not listening. "She left, Ken. And I fucking let her. Kris has lived her life for other people. Making choices for herself with them in mind. Doing what she thinks will benefit them over herself. I won't be another person she does that for Ken. I can't do that to her. What am I supposed to do?"

"This isn't the same as any of that, and you know it. Fight for her, Carter. Go get our girl and bring her home."

The way he says it calms my beating heart. It's like I hadn't thought that was even a possibility...

"Go get her and bring her home?" I ask slowly. I throw my hat onto the porch and pull at my hair. "Just, go and get her?" The more I say it, the less insane it sounds.

"Yeah, pal. Go and get her." Ken laughs a little bit.

I pause my pacing and hair pulling and look at the swing. I make my way over to it and pick up the book she left. The book she forgot. It has a corner of a bookmark sticking out, so I open the book and lean back against the railing.

Her bookmark is a picture. A four by six printed photo. It's of the three of us. Cameron is in the middle, mine and Kris' cheeks pressing in on his making his lips pucker a bit like a little fish. And on the back, in her simple handwriting, it says "*my loves*". Her smile is wide and my heart stops. She looks so happy. So good and loved. I thought she was beautiful the first second I laid eyes on her almost six years ago. But this picture, this stupidly simple selfie... My goodness. She's fucking gorgeous when she's happy.

"Happy looks good on her," Ken says from my right.

I look up at him and close the book, leaving the picture where it was.

"I've got to go get her, Ken."

He puts a hand on my shoulder and laughs. "I'll drive you to the airport."

The earliest flight was out of Omaha. Ken drove me to the airport and after one stop and eight hours, an Uber ride given by a twenty-two-year-old with long brown hair that looked like Shaggy from Scooby-Doo, and a whole lot of mental preparation on what I am going to say— I am finally standing in front of Bryce and Sherry's one story, blue house in Fargo.

I shake my hands out, take a deep breath, and pull my phone out of my pocket. I click on *"Kris With The Good Ass"* and on what feels like the four thousandth ring she answers.

"Carter? Are you okay?"

"I'm standing outside your brother's house."

"What?" she all but yells.

After a moment of silence, I say again, "I'm standing outside."

"But," she says slowly, "I'm standing outside of *your* house."

My heart drops to my gut and then back to my throat.

"You're fucking kidding?"

She laughs as she opens the front door, three yards away from me. "Yeah," she says, "I am fucking kidding."

I can see the tears from here but neither of us moves as we pocket our phones.

I hold out her book. It is light pink and thick. "You forgot this."

I take a few steps towards her, and she does the same. There is three feet separating us now and it's three feet too much. But I will *not* scare her. Not now, not again.

"Come home." I say softly. "We don't have to do the whole farm family thing if you don't want to. If it's too much. We don't need chickens. Or goats. And I can work the cows alone like I always have. Harvest time will suck for you, but I promise it's short lived." My words come out fast like if I don't get them all out, Kris might disappear without hearing me say them. "Just come home. The dog misses you. Cam misses you. I fucking need you, sweetheart."

"You think I left because of cows and chickens?" She raises her eyebrows and takes another step.

"We'll I don't-"

"Carter Arlington Francis Barker." One more step towards me, leaving a foot between us. "I did not leave because of those... those... *things*." She shakes her head. "I left because of me. Because I am damaged goods. Because I can't give Cameron a brother or a sister someday. I can't even pretend that that breaks my heart for me at this point because it's all I know now and I'm fine with it. I left because I'm terrified that someday you'll wake up and Cameron won't have tiny little toes or say 'dine-saur' anymore and you'll miss that and want more and then see me for what I am— broken. At least in that regard. Unable to provide you with more. And I don't want to have established a whole life with you, with Cameron," her voice breaks on his name. "Just for you to turn around one day and realize that I am not good enough for you and your life."

I am taken aback by her admission. It's not that it's surprising. It is just completely insane.

"Carter-"

"Nope," I cut her off and close the space between us. "My turn." I carefully set her book on the ground next to us and take her hands in mine. Her nails are not painted and now that I look at her more closely, I see the darkness under her eyes and the way her hair looks like she hasn't been brushing it like I know she loves to. Her face is a little thinner and my heart breaks. "Come. Home. It's your home.

I'm your home. *Cameron* is your home. You think I want more kids? I don't. I didn't want Cameron until Cameron became a someone. I have never been happier than I am with you and him. The three of us. And I have never been as miserable as I am without you, Kris. Fuck, I have been drowning in my own sorrow, missing you day in and day out. And then I saw you, just now and here, and it's like a piece of me is finally as it should be again. Cameron asks about you every day. We love you. We *want* you. We need you." I take a breath and put my forehead on hers. "Come home, sweetheart. Please. Don't be afraid of things that aren't going to happen, and don't think for another second that the parts of you that are slightly fractured aren't wholly and irrevocably loved by me."

The silence stretches between us, each breath somehow coming easier than the last. Her hands grip my wrists as I hold her face in mine. She pulls her head back and looks at me. I am taken back to a similar moment in our room two weeks ago, right before she walked out of our home. But she does not pull away this time. She looks at me. Really, truly looks at me. Like she's searching for answers I would give her, she would only need to ask.

Then she whispers something that does finally take me out at the knees.

"Okay."

I drop. My knees give out with sheer relief. She holds my head to her stomach, running her fingers through my hair after taking my hat off and tossing it by her book. I let it all go. I am not typically a crier, and after the day Kris left, I had not cried again. It didn't matter that my heart was shattered, that my world was dark. But now, with her holding me and telling me yes— I cry.

After a moment of holding me, she drops to her own knees in front of me and takes my face in her hands. She kisses my forehead and my cheeks, the bridge of my nose and the just above my lips, her thumbs swiping at my tears.

She whispers to me, breathing life back into me, "I love you, Carter."

I don't let her go. Not her hips or her hair or her hand. Not while she packs or says goodbye to her brother and Sherry, or on the drive back home. I might never stop the need to feel her again, not even for a second.

I look over at her as I drive us home. She showered before getting in the car. Her dark hair is down and half wet, curling slightly in random spots. The golden pieces are all fading and disappearing. I brush it over her shoulder and work the muscles there.

"No chickens then?" I ask her.

Her eyes shoot to mine, nearly scared, and I laugh.

"Carter," she says seriously. "No chickens at home. Like, ever."

Home.

"No chickens, sweetheart. Just the big white cows you like so much."

Epilogue

Mom

Fifteen Years Later

Kris

The house is bustling with family and friends. There are people outside on the grass and in the driveway, some inside chatting in the living room and kitchen. Long white tables are everywhere. Inside there is one for gifts and cards. On the driveway there are three filled with food. Crockpots of meatballs and sliced ham. Casserole dishes filled with different sides like cheesy potatoes and green beans and whatever else I thought anyone might like. There are brownies and cookies and a cake with Cameron's little baby face on it.

And a banner hanging from the columns of the porch saying "Happy Graduation Cam" in bright gold letters.

"You did good, sweetheart."

The whisper hits my cheek at the same time *his* lips do.

"I just wanted it to be perfect for him." I spin around and put my hands around Carter's waist, pulling him close to me.

Gosh, he ages well. His beard that he grows out now is more than half gray. His dark hair, that somehow is not thinning, looks like it has tiny slivers of sparkles sprinkled throughout, making up half the color. He loves when I describe them as such, obviously. The lines and creases that have shown up in the last fifteen years all move as he smiles at me. But it is his eyes that always do me in, even now. They are the same bright but deep blue they were all those years ago when we met for the first time in a dimly lit arena in South Dakota.

"It's beyond perfect, Kris." Carter kisses the tip of my nose and holds me close to him.

"Cameron is having fun." I nod my head towards our kid.

Our grown kid.

Cameron has grown into the most incredible man. He is tall, an inch or so over six foot. His hair is the perfect shade of dark brown and he keeps it just long enough to be able to swoop it across his head like he likes to do. He's tan, now, like his dad. The once-pale skin grew into that gene, apparently.

He does not say 'dine-saur' anymore, though. At that thought, my eyes start to burn slightly. I rest my cheek on Carter's chest and sigh.

He must be able to feel us looking at him. He smiles widely at us and says something to the group of friends he is standing with by the corn hole boards. His long, blue jean clad legs carry him to where his dad and I are hugging. In the next breath his arms are thrown around us both.

"Great party, ma," he says to me, popping a big loud kiss on the top of my head.

The first time he called me mom I about had a stroke. I was caught somewhere between panic for hurting Sadie somehow and also bliss because it is all I ever dreamed of for his and my relationship.

But he had already asked Sadie if I could share that title with her and she happily said yes. I love that woman.

Cameron takes a step back and digs in his pocket. His face turns a little nervous and Carter moves a step away from me.

"You okay, Camy?" I ask him, setting my hand on his forearm.

He smiles at me and holds out a little purple baggy. "Yeah, I'm good. I got you something."

"*Me*?" I put my hands on my chest. "It's your party. You shouldn't be giving me anything."

"It's also Mother's Day weekend. So, deal with it," he teases and shrugs.

I laugh and roll my eyes. "I do love presents."

"We know," my boys say together before laughing.

I open the small bag and tip it over. A small gasp leaves me as a beautiful ring falls into my palm. It's silver and a little thick, the perfect size for my right ring finger. The stone is a square purple amethyst, Cameron's birthstone, and it catches the sun as I move it around on my hand.

"Cam," I say as I look up at him. "It's stunning."

"it's a mother's ring," he says proudly.

Tears fill my eyes as I put my hand on Cameron's cheek.

"It's engraved, too. On the inside."

I quickly pull the ring off, excited to see what it says.

"09.17.23."

I look up at him and smile widely. "Is this the day I first got to meet you?"

His smile explodes and he nods. "Dad and I tracked the exact date down through random photos and really, really old text messages he found on an old phone."

We both smile at Carter.

"This is the best gift I have ever received, Cameron. Thank you, honey. I love it." I hug him tightly. "And I love you so much."

"It's the date you became my mom. Even if I didn't call you that yet." He pulls back. "I'm so glad you chose us. That you chose me."

The tears flow this time. Not just from me, either. Cameron is crying. Carter is crying. Sadie comes over and is crying. By the time we all dry our cheeks Lance has made it over and sheds a couple tears. We all start to laugh as we dry our eyes.

Cameron puts one arm around my shoulders and his other around Sadie's, pulling us into his sides.

"Dad," he calls out. "Take a picture of me with my moms."

Sadie and I smile at each other.

"And then have Uncle Kenny come over to take a picture of the whole family."

The whole family.

Once upon a time I did not think I would have this. A family like this. A son and a husband and a best friend and her husband, and a whole town of support and love. It wasn't all easy but it was all worth it.

"And then I saw you" I think to myself as I watch Carter make his way to my other side.

I look at Sadie and Lance, and then Cameron. Carter throws his arm around me and puts his hand on Cam's shoulder.

He leans in and kisses the side of my head.

"I love you, Carter."

"I love you too, sweetheart."

Recipe for Carter's Aunt's "Mexican Meatloaf"

Ingredients

2lbs ground beef

2 10.5oz cans Cream of Mushroom soup

1 6oz can of Tomato Paste

1 16oz jar of mild Taco Sauce

3/4 cup of uncooked Minute Rice

2 cups of crushed Doritos

Shredded Mexican Blend Cheese

To Cook

Heat oven to 350 degrees. Brown the ground beef and drain grease. Mix the beef, cream of mushroom soup, tomato paste, taco sauce, and uncooked rice together in the pan or a bowl. Pour half of the beef mixture into a deep 9x6-ish baking dish. Layer the crushed Doritos over top. Pour the remaining beef mixture on top of those. Sprinkle shredded cheese over the top of that. Bake uncovered for 30-40 minutes. Let cool for 5-10 minutes and serve.

Acknowledgements

This book was beyond fun to write. The story is wild and silly and "unhinged" and that was the goal. I wanted this to be something that was just insane enough to be nearly out of this world, but also still real enough to feel... *real*. And I think And Then I Saw You. did the job. Compared to my first book, I'll Never Be., ATISY. is more light and airy. A solid palette cleanser, if you will. Even for me as the writer.

To my husband, my guy, my very own *Farm Daddy*. Thank you for answering all of my questions about whether or not John Deere makes balers and how to phrase sentences about irrigation motors. I love you. I love our cows. I love our life. I stand firm on the no chickens thing though.

To my sweet angel baby doll girls. I love you both to pieces. If you read anything I write someday, I hope you do so with pride, and also laughter. I only ever want to be someone you're proud of.

And to the real angel baby that we never got to meet, the inspiration behind some of the more graphic and sad moments in this book... I loved you then and I love you now.

To my book-writing Fairy Godmother, ABH— look ma! No hands. I love you, truly.

To my early readers for hyping me up and helping me improve upon what I had already written. Jenah, Emily, Lena, Dora, Amber, Samantha, Chelsea, Cassie, Holly... you guys. I don't know what I would do without all of the comments and the recommendations and the love. I love you all to pieces. Thank you, thank you, thank you.

To my friends and family that never make me feel anything other than loved and supported, thank you.

And to you. Yes honey, *you*. Thank you for reading ATISY. and giving her, and me, a shot. I love you.

xoxo

A. L. Fox

About the Author

A. L. Fox is an indie author, though she feels weird calling herself the "a" word. She spends her days with her two small children and her farmer husband. She enjoys 70 degree weather and rain, Starbucks and Target, and laughing. A. L. Fox was born and raised in the Midwest and likes to think her writing will reach who it needs to. She plans to continue to create but has no real, big goals while doing so. She's thankful everyday for the chance to do this whole *thing*.

Her main goal: bring joy to others.

Also By

I'll Never Be.

I Wish.

9 798218 321536